NOAH GATES

A CHRISTIAN WESTERN

REG QUIST

Noah Gates
Reg Quist

CKN Christian Publishing
An Imprint of Wolfpack Publishing
6032 Wheat Penny Avenue
Las Vegas, NV 89122

ISBN: 978-1-64119-050-3

NOAH GATES

NOAH

"Hello the fire."

"I seen you. No need to waken the dead with your shout'n. If you're look'n for directions, I don't have any that are apt to help you get to where you're going. If you're look'n for coffee, tie your rides over there away from the camp and bring your cups. But come peaceful. And just to make sure you do, I'd appreciate if you'd hang your gun belts to your saddle horns."

I'm a peaceful man. Most times anyway. But I've found it to be better all the way around if everyone understands the rules right from the get-go. One of the rules I kind of like is for me to be the one with the weapon to hand when dealing with strangers. More peaceful that way, you might say. So I said my piece, looked up at the rider from where I sat leaning against a willow bush with my carbine laying across my legs, and waited.

A big, bearded man wearing filthy much-worn and

slept-in range clothes with a patterned poncho pulled over his head and a weather-destroyed hat pulled low onto his ears grimaced through a forest of hair. "I ain't had this gun belt off for many a day, stranger. Were I to do as you say, how do I know you won't up and shoot us first chance you got?"

I looked at his filthy pants and was pretty sure he told the truth about not having taken off the belt for some long time or the pants, either one. "If my intention was to shoot you, there would already be blood on the grass. But you suit yourselves. Hang them up or ride on. I ain't all that lonesome for company so it makes no never mind to me."

Bushy Face and his skinny, equally filthy partner looked at each other and rode to tie their horses. I saw a look pass between them. I wasn't sure just exactly what it meant but they hung up their cartridge belts, dug tin cups out of bulging saddlebags and approached the fire. None of us offered our names.

They both squatted down by the fire and picked up the coffeepot which I had nudged towards them with the toe of my boot. I was drawing dangerously close to the last of my coffee but, on the trail, folks just naturally share. I kind of knotted up inside though as I watched those two dirty cups filling with my scarce brew. Bushy Face went back to his saddlebag and returned with a handful of jerky. He held out maybe the dirtiest hand I've ever laid eyes on and offered me some of the dried meat.

"Thanks, no. I ate the most of a rabbit I knocked over with a rock this afternoon so I've had a-plenty." I'd have eaten that rabbit raw, or nothing at all, rather than bite into that dried meat offering.

Well, I figured I'd done my duty when I gave them the expected Western welcome pushing the pot that held the most of the last of my coffee towards them. I owed them nothing else.

I took a long look at the two and found it hard to believe they both had mothers at one time in the past. I figured the mothers would hang their heads in shame if they were to see their sons now.

But then the thought flashed through my mind that my own mother, were she still alive, might have a question or two for me to answer. It's almost like I could hear her asking, "Noah Gates, why are you wasting your life chasing gone horses. Months living like a vagabond and you haven't found a single animal. They're stolen and gone."

Well, there was a bit more to the story than that. Still, I knew she was right. But if a man wished to look himself in the mirror he had to at least try to find those that took what wasn't theirs to take.

Anyway, I had kind of grown to enjoy the wandering although what had caused me to ride so far north was a question I didn't have a ready answer for.

As I was riding, a part of my mind had been working on a plan that required the end of snow and winter and the sprouting of spring grass.

It's a difficult thing, starting over. Many a man has done it but it was new to me and I had to think some before settling on a firm plan. I figured I could think and ride at the same time so I had been riding, just seeing the lay of the land. Mind you, I could have ridden into warmer country but it was too late to change that.

Spring in the Rocky Mountain high country, which was where I was headed, was still weeks away so I was in no special hurry.

I looked over at the two camp guests who had made themselves at home beside my fire.

"You boys figure to move on?"

"I guess tomorrow would be soon enough to move out," answered Bushy Face. "Our horses have done some miles today and would benefit from the rest. You mind if we roll our blankets out here?"

I gestured in no particular direction with a lift of my chin. "Free country," I said. "You could take your rest over nearer your horses. I've got a dog running with me. Gets nervous with too many folks around. You don't want to be on his bad side."

Skinny spoke for the first time, "I don't see no dog."

"He's off catching his supper. You'll see him. All in good time."

They went to picket their horses where the animals could graze the winter-killed grass and water at a little trickle of snow melt that had attracted me earlier in the afternoon. That trickle of water had been the reason for my stopping where I did. Then they rolled out their beds on the Dakota grass before coming back to the fire. We talked the evening twilight into full dark, saying nothing at all that mattered or would be remembered.

They selfishly drank my coffeepot dry, which should have been a warning to me of what kind of men they were, and then went to their bedrolls. The dog returned from his solitary hunt. After sniffing around the strange horses and men for a few minutes, he came and lay down beside the fire.

When I woke the next morning with daylight only a faint promise in the east, the two riders were saddling up, seemingly in a hurry. They must have moved almighty quiet and careful for me not have heard them when they first started rustling around.

I sat up on one elbow, placed my hat on my head and reached under my blanket for my Colt. I figured the dog had left camp again on a hunt for his breakfast or he would have growled a warning at me.

"You boys are saddled up early."

"Well, we had a good sleep and the horses are rested. No use burn'n daylight. Need to thank you for the coffee. We'll be on our way."

They took off out of there as if they could hear their mothers calling them, or more likely some far off sheriff.

I pushed my blanket aside and stood up in my sock feet. I scratched away a nighttime itch and stretched some of the hard ground out of my bones. After looking to see that both of my horses were still staked out and there was no sign of trouble in the gathering dawn, I reached for my pants.

After I was dressed and preparing for the trail, I discovered my leather poke with half my traveling money in it was gone. I had the other half safely buried deep in my offside pannier. Those boys had lifted that poke right out of my coat pocket which was draped over my saddle.

Now what kind of men would repay my kindness that way? And me, a gentle and peace-loving man most times, unless aggravated or provoked like I already told you.

It wasn't until I had made up the last of my coffee, adding it to the dregs from the night before, eaten some leftover biscuits and started to pack my gear that I discovered the poke was gone. By that time the thieves were down the trail by a good bit. Well, I would say I was some provoked so I saddled up and set out after them. But with two horses to rig out, plus all my earthly belongings needing to be packed into their panniers and tied to the back of my packhorse, a good bit of time had gone by. Still, I set out with grim determination.

I followed them for a ways, their tracks leaving clods of turned up sod behind them. No one would ever accuse my packhorse of being fast on his feet so I knew the thieves were making headway on me. Judging by how far those clods were scattered from where they were torn out of the ground, I judged they were surely making miles across the North Dakota countryside.

Until I was robbed and had taken up the chase of the two thieves, I had been enjoying my aimless ride in the cool, spring weather. Well now, that's not just exactly the whole entire truth. The fact is that my ride was only aimless up to a point. It's true that I had no exact destination but I did have a purpose even if the details were a bit slow in finding their way out of my mind. My purpose was also becoming a bit dimmer as time went on.

The other fact is that this was the second time I had been robbed and I didn't enjoy the experience any more than I had the first time.

The first loss had been my entire herd of G-bar trade horses. That had been the most of a year ago so those horses could be almost anywhere by now, sold off to twenty different buyers. I had mostly given them up for lost months ago although I still watched the brands of animals that came into view.

Oh, I looked for those horses alright. Don't ever think I didn't. But this is a big country and by the time I decided the thieves had taken a different direction than what I had guessed there was no more trail to follow.

After that theft, I had been left still owning the livery barn and a small freight outfit in that little one street town so back I went. I settled down to haul freight for the rest of the summer months knowing in my heart that the search for my G-bar horses was hopeless.

I've met men who wasted a big part of their lives chasing one thing or another with nothing to show at the end of the trail. It had been a lesson to me.

When the chance came, I sold the barn and freight outfit and decided I had enough money left to keep body and soul together for a few months so, having nothing at all holding me, I set out to see some country.

Chasing these two camp thieves had not been in my original plan and neither was the dramatic change in the weather I could see boiling in from the northwest. The first lightning struck so close it caused my horse to shy and nearly dump me on the ground. The thunder that followed stopped both animals dead in their tracks.

The light show in the sky lasted for several minutes and then the skies opened. I was soaked through in the first minute. The thieves' tracks I had been following led onto a patch of rocky ground; short grass struggling its way through a generous layer of gravel. Poor country for tracking in or for much of anything else when it comes to that. What few tracks that were left soon washed away under the wet onslaught.

I gave it up after a few miles, hoping to see the thieves again somewhere down the trail where I would have a word or two to say to them. So I pulled up in the most likely place for a camp, as poor as it was, and settled in for the night.

I had known there was going to be a change in the weather when those great, black thunderheads started rolling across the heavens, darkening the sky and turning the grasslands into a shadowy, scary place for a lone rider. Those black clouds seemed to roll over and change places with the gray clouds from lower down and then rise into the air once more only to fall and roll over again.

The first flash of lightening took but a split second to travel from those low-lying clouds to the waiting earth. Its brilliant flash of light caused me to blink my eyes and my horse stopped dead in his tracks. I would swear I smelled brimstone but that might have been my imagination again or the remembrance of warnings heard long ago in our hill country meeting house when I was a boy.

The flash of lightening was followed by low, rumbling thunder that worked its way into a roll of sound that shook the earth and the very soul of anyone foolish enough to be traveling horseback as I was.

If you ain't ever seen a prairie storm, you likely don't understand what I'm telling you. A prairie storm has a way of grabbing your attention. I mean your concentration becomes honed down to just the one thing as the sky lights up and the ground beneath your feet trembles.

The lightning and thunder lasted only a couple of hours but the rain continued for three long, miserable days. There's just no shelter at all worth talking about on that bald prairie except what a few clumps of aspen offer and maybe a spruce tree or two. I tried to make the best of the situation, gaining only a few miles during the day and seeking new shelter each night. I had no idea at all where I might find a town.

On the third morning of rain, after giving up on any more sleep, I pushed my wet blanket to the side and sat up, reaching to where my hat could be picked off the aspen twig I had hung it on. I shook some of the gathered rain from the sagging, travel-weary Stetson and fit it down over my long still-damp hair. I pulled my boots over my bare feet, the saturated leather grabbing my skin at every tug. I had dropped my last pair of wet socks onto my campfire the night before, judging them as beyond the help of needle and thread.

Gathering twigs and dead branches to get a fire going the night before had been no easy task with the rain having pretty well soaked the countryside. I didn't figure to repeat the effort for a morning fire since I had used up the last pinch of my coffee the day before. Anything I might have cooked up from my dwindling supplies wasn't worth the effort.

I had slept with my clothes on as wet as they were so standing up, hat and boots in place, I was as ready for the day as I was likely to get. Anyone looking on would have found little to impress them except maybe my size. I'm a big man, standing just over six feet without my boots, and broad of shoulder. I'm stronger for work than most men and although I avoid trouble if possible, my size seems to be a challenge to some men. Situations like that a man does what has to be done.

No girl ever called me handsome but none ever ran from the sight of me either so you can take from that whatever you wish.

My soaked gear was soon rolled and tied in its pannier on my packhorse with me shivering in the pre-dawn cold, all the time thinking about California, a place I'd heard about but wasn't apt to ever see.

The cowboy tales told around campfires and in lonesome, rangeland bunkhouses surely made California sound like a warm, inviting place to be. None of those old boys had ever actually been all the way west to California but each of them seemed to have a firm opinion on its wonders anyway.

It was said that the sun shines every day in California. Nothing in my experience led me to believe that such a thing was even possible so it could have been just idle talk. Cowboy talk.

Lonesome men leaning against their saddles around the evening fire, their tin plates loaded with the usual beans, beef and biscuits at the end of a long, cold day of riding, will say nearly anything just for the want of hearing another human voice. Some of the things a body would hear wouldn't stand up to close examination but, in situations like that, a man has to make allowance.

It's a long ride from Dakota to California and one I'm not likely to ever make. But a day like this you can't blame a man for dreaming a bit.

One thing for sure was that there was no hint of sun or even a weak sunrise on this dreary, wet, North Dakota morning. And it was silent. I didn't hear a sound from any direction except for the still-falling rain. Even the birds and normally grass-shuffling critters had given up on the day, and the day hadn't even really begun yet.

I could picture the birds poking their heads over the lip of their nests and thinking, 'Forget it, I ain't that hungry' and snuggling back into their cozy hideaways. But then, I'm given to idle imaginings from time to time.

I brushed as much water as I could off the back of my horse and saddled up. Then I unrolled my gun belt from the oilskin I kept it in overnight and buckled it on. I palmed the Colt and rotated the cylinder after checking the loads, a habit gained from hard experience over the years. The weapon was nearly lost in my big hand, making it awkward to hold and shoot. I had come to depend more on my carbine but I could still make the old, worn Colt sing a happy tune when the need came.

My carbine was hanging from the stub of a broken branch, the barrel pointed down to keep the rain out with the green, budding spread of branches above somewhat sheltering it. I wiped it off with the flat of my hand and slid it into the scabbard after taking a final look over the country to assure myself that I had no immediate need for its use.

The rain continued to fall. Not a sprinkle such as you might enjoy if you and your best girl were out for a ride, snuggled under a buggy top with a lap robe to keep you warm. No, this was a full on downpour; a rain that would melt the last of the prairie snow that was hidden away in shady places and water the waiting roots of the thirsty grass.

I had managed very little sleep in my wet bed but there was no point in staying any longer in the aspen grove so I swung into the saddle and kicked the reluctant horse into motion. "Noah Gates," I said to myself, "if someone was to ask you what you were doing out here, wet and lost on the prairie, you'd really be stuck for an answer. So best you find somewhere else to be. Preferably somewhere dry."

Soaked to the skin and dumb with loss of sleep, we lit out to exactly where I didn't know. This was all strange country to me but there was a clear trail that others had made along the rise of a bank above a small river that I took to be the Pembina. That trail followed along just fine, heading more or less west I thought, eventually rising up the slope of a hillside until I was looking a fair ways down into the valley of the river.

I no longer knew for sure which direction was which. I hadn't seen the sun in three days and the compass in my head had quit working.

2

NOAH

THE RIDING WAS good in spite of the rain so I dozed off in the saddle, trusting to Sam, my bay gelding, which probably says more about my wisdom than it does about the horse. But we had been over some hills and through some creeks together, that horse and I, and I felt he had earned the trust. And I surely was feeling that lack of sleep. So I nodded my head, slumped in the saddle and dozed. The packhorse would follow without trouble and Wolf, that big ugly dog that had taken up with me, was happy as long as we were moving.

We followed an eyebrow of a trail along the bank of the Pembina River at a place I found out later was known by the locals as the Pembina Gorge.

You ever seen those banks? Steep. Steep and scary they are. Not too far off the vertical and all yellow clay with here and there a scattered growth of bush clinging to life while holding a sparse bit of soil from sliding into the waiting river. After a good rain, that yellow clay turns to a slippery soup that nothing can stand up in.

Well, we rode along that trail and it was surely raining. Everything was soaked including that five-hundred-foot drop to the river. Senseless with loss of sleep, I was trusting to Sam to stay to the trail but he lost his footing going through a little draw where run-off water had cut through the lip of the bank. Maybe he was sleepy, too.

It would seem that a thinking kind of a horse would be able to stay to a simple trail; but Sam, he lost his footing. First his hind legs kind of skittered sideways, that yellow clay offering him no footing at all. Then he slid backwards a bit losing his balance. I was startled full awake by that time. Next thing I know we're sliding sideways and only about three feet from the edge of that bank.

"Whoa," I hollered. "Whoa!"

Even a deaf horse would have heard the panic in my voice but he paid not the slightest attention. He slid and fought for balance until the fool actually turned and, looking for firm footing, lunged towards the riverbank.

Well, I hollered "Whoa" again but he didn't do it. It was far too late anyway. We crashed through some small aspen and willow bushes, and his front feet fell over the lip of that bank.

"Now you've went and gone and done it," I hollered. "I think you done that a purpose." Well, he stood there for a split second - his hind feet on the trail and his front feet in midair - and the next thing I know we're headed down that greasy slope of yellow clay and there ain't noth'n to slow us down all the way to the bottom. I just had time to cast off the lead rope so Rascal wouldn't be dragged down with us. Rascal though, fool that he is, followed. Right to the bottom, kicking and jumping and sliding.

From time to time over the weeks of travel, I had tired of holding the lead rope and turned Rascal loose, thinking he would follow. But it wasn't long before he would find something of interest and turn to one side or the other and I'd have to go back and pick up the rope again. But this time he followed, straight over the ridge of that riverbank and onto that wet yellow clay. Wolf followed right along, too.

Sitting up in the middle of that horse allowed me a clear view of the river and all the country around. Fear like I had never felt before kept me from appreciating the full beauty of it right at that moment though.

Sam had his head down and his front feet spread wide apart to try to stop himself. "A little late to think of that," I yelled at him.

I had my feet jammed into the stirrups so hard it's a wonder I didn't tear them from the saddle. Anyway, we picked up speed and headed for the river. I heard someone screaming in terror. It might have been me.

Ol' Sam, he slid some and then he took a couple of jumps and slid some more. Along about the middle of that bank there was a big growth of bushes; willow and chokecherry and such. We went right through the thickest of them, taking on considerable scratches and scrapes from the branches. One long, slim branch gave me an awful whap across the face but I felt nothing until later.

Sam, he didn't slow down one bit. When he leaped over the last of the willow bunch, I thought he might sprout wings and fly clear across the river; he landed running and then put his front feet out again and skidded. I lost my hat somewhere.

I figured we were moving faster than the settler trains bringing folks out from the east. All we lacked was the whistle. And a way of stopping.

The idea of reaching the bottom started to become a concern to me. There was just nowhere for a horse to stop, nowhere at all that didn't offer a broken leg or worse. The riverbank was wide and flat with a jumble of round rocks as big as your head lying freely on a bed of sand and mud.

There was, here and there along the shore, a stunted spruce and some bushes that could live through the spring floods. It was poor walking at the best of times and no place at all for a horse and rider.

Just as I was thinking that nothing in this world had ever moved so fast on the back of a horse, Rascal passed us and then Wolf leaped past. They were leading a fast sliding mess of mud and rock and broken branches. My pack with all my worldly possessions was hanging under Rascal. I didn't have time to worry about it though.

That river was coming fast to meet us and I had worked up some serious doubts about how this trip was going to end. I was as scared as I've ever been but I didn't recognize that fact until later after I'd had time to think about it.

Sam must have been worried too because he started to fight it. He leaped and slid and went sideways. I didn't fall off until just a few feet short of the bottom. First I lost one stirrup and then I started to bounce. I bounced twice in the saddle and once on the horse's rump. I finally let loose of my death grip on the horn and dropped over Sam's tail. An iron-shod hoof glanced off my shoulder and then Sam and I went our separate ways.

The first thing that hit that yellow clay was my left foot. I felt something give with a terrible shock of pain and then I flopped over onto my hind end and finished the ride down that way, my slide slowed by a gathering pile of yellow gumbo in front of my boots and between my legs.

Digging my boot heels in as hard as I could, I finally

pulled up against the first row of boulders at the river's edge and came to a welcome stop.

Rascal started to run as he neared the bottom and ran right into that rain swollen river, taking my pack with him. How he got through those rocks without breaking a leg I'll never know.

Sam got himself turned a little and ran along the mud and rocks at the river's edge. Wolf slid and plunged all the way and seemed to enjoy the experience.

When I settled to a stop at the bottom, I just sat there with that wet, yellow clay soaking into my britches and with my heart pounding like a trip hammer.

My long, oiled-canvas riding coat was wrapped every which way around my middle. I pulled my knees up and lay my head on them for a while, wet and shaking but alive. The movement brought back the pain of my wrenched knee and I had to straighten out my leg again.

Unbidden visions of home and comfort flashed through my mind and the question of what I was doing out here. Then I remembered that my old home was no more nor were the people who had made it a welcoming place.

The broken health that followed my father home from the war, topped off with poverty and a hacking cough that just wouldn't quit, had finally put 'paid' to his life.

Mother followed him to the grave a few weeks later, her spirits and her health both broken. My two brothers, my sister, and I all pulled out and went our separate ways.

Even two decades after the events I knew my family was victim to the price of war still being paid by those who had worn a uniform and carried arms.

Wolf came over and licked my face. I pushed him away after ruffling his neck hair a bit. Rascal was still floundering around in the river dragging my pack so I finally got up and led him to the shore, favoring my left knee and trying to ignore the pain. Sam came back limping a little. Wolf was running around wagging his tail like this had all been a game and he was ready to do it again.

A lightening flash and a rumble of thunder reminded me that it was still raining.

It took me an hour or more to get everything straightened out moving as slow as I was with pain and misery added to the wet and the lack of sleep. There was nowhere dry to spread out my pack and no sign of a let up in the rain so I reloaded everything wet and set out to find a way up that slope.

But first I cleaned my guns on my shirttail which was the only more or less dry piece of cloth I could find. I wasn't expecting trouble but a man never really knew. It paid to be careful. And ready.

I removed the cartridges, cleaned the weapons and then each shell before reloading the pieces. I managed to use my coat to protect my Colt from the rain but the carbine was exposed to the weather.

A slow five mile walk dodging river water and half-submerged boulders with both Sam and me limping more painfully the further we went took me to flatter ground and lower riverbanks. A short, difficult scramble with me hanging on to Sam's tail to assist my climb took the animals and me out of the river valley and onto the trail above, probably the same trail we'd been following before.

A mile or so ahead, I could see a scattering of buildings. They didn't look like much but some folks must call them 'home'. The sight of stove smoke struggling to rise against the falling rain was a welcome promise of a hot meal and a warm bed.

The walk had been frustratingly slow due to Sam's limp which seemed to get a little worse with each mile traveled.

I wasn't doing much better myself. I swung onto his back and rode for a short while to rest my knee but guilt and the fear of hurting him more made me step back to the ground.

The lack of sleep and food was struggling against my injured knee to see which could cause me the more misery.

Did I mention that it was raining?

I limped around a corral that housed a dozen or so droop-headed horses, their backs shiny with rainwater. I went close enough to see there were no G-bar's burned into their hides before leading my two animals into the livery stable. Checking brands was a habit I had picked up the year before during my long hopeless hunt for the stolen trade horses.

I caught an amused grin from the hostler although he made no move to rise from the rickety chair he had tipped back against the wall. "Wet 'nuff fer ya, young feller? Slow goin' what with that bay limping the way he is. You ain't looking too spry yer own self neither. Saw ya com'n. Figured ta be ready so I put a bait of oats in that there double-stall." He pointed with his chin, never once pulling his hands from the pockets of his bib overalls. "Lots of hay."

He looked at me from the dry shelter of the stable, the beginnings of a smile with a question attached threatening to split his whiskers apart. "Most folks wear some headgear."

I'd have normally answered with a grin and a smart comment but I didn't have it in me this day. I shrugged my shoulders which caused a small cascading of water to drip from my hair. "Hat fell off and I didn't have time to go searching for it. Wasn't really much of a hat anymore anyway but I kind of had a fondness for it just the same."

I stalled the animals and slipped the bridle and saddle

from Sam, half-carrying, half-dragging the heavy stock rig into the tack room, favoring my knee. The room held three other outfits and a rack of harness.

Wolf lay down on the fresh straw between the horses as he liked to do. He would make that his home until we saddled up again, taking it upon himself to see that no harm came to the beasts.

I untied the packs and lay one down in the runway while the hostler did the same with the other. I lugged the packsaddle into the tack room and pointed back at the panniers. "Can I leave those with you until I find a place to settle for a day or two?"

His answer was to pick a pannier up and drop it in the corner of his small office. I followed with the other.

We walked together to the big entry doors and stood silently looking at the rain. The town's single street was a quagmire of mud and refuse at least ankle deep and deeper in spots with a tangle of wagon tracks cutting every which way.

On one side of the street was the gunsmith and saddle shop sitting tightly beside the sheriff's office with its small jail, plus a miscellaneous group of shacks and a large farm supply store. Across the street, the row of tired buildings included a print shop, a saloon with a few horses tied off and standing in the rain, a mercantile, a generously-sized cafe and a small hotel.

There were raised wooden walks on both sides of the street mostly covered by overhangs on each business building. I could see a scattering of small houses carelessly spread out over the prairie, each with an outhouse, a small barn or shed and a corral. There was just nothing at all that was inviting enough for a long stay or anything to help improve my frame of mind except the promise of a hot meal. Of course, that meal was on the other side of that muddy quagmire of a road. I figured that was about equal to the happenings of the rest of that day.

I was wet misery through and through and coming close to feeling sorry for myself.

The hostler rightly judged my thinking. "Ain't no two ways about it, young feller. Yu'r here and the hotel and cafe is over there with that strip of wet muck between. No way to get there but one step at a time so you got 'er to do." Then he chuckled as if I was there for his personal amusement.

I grinned a sickly grin at him. "Wet as I am and as muddy, that short walk won't make hardly any difference at all. I'll be back later after I take on some feed. Obliged if you could find time to give those horses a rubdown and try to get some of the mud off their legs. Normally I would care for my animals before myself but this time they're just going to have to be patient. They've been eating wet grass while I've done without anything at all."

"I'll find some liniment for that bay's leg, too."

I thanked him and said, "I'll be back shortly after I've eaten. Give you a hand with the horses."

I had taken maybe a dozen slow steps, the mud and filth grabbing and sucking at my boots with the rain pounding on my bare head, when the saloon doors burst open and the two men who had stolen my poke stumbled out assisted by the barkeeper who had a hand on each of their coat collars. Some harsh words were exchanged that I couldn't hear clearly and the two staggered through the mud to the hitch rail and climbed onto their wet saddles, laughing and jeering at the barman. A collection of saloon hangers-on had followed them out to the sidewalk balancing their drinks in their hands and chuckling at the show.

They wheeled around and kicked their horses into a lope in the direction of the stable.

Then Bushy Face pulled to a sliding stop, glaring at me and calling to his skinny sidekick. He laughed and pointed, shouting slurred words, "Hey, there's that pilgrim, soaked and muddy and on foot. Saddest sight I ever did see. Let's go say howdy." Whatever questionable wisdom their mothers left them with was lost in a haze of whisky fumes.

Totally misjudging the situation, they filled the air with rebel yells that brought folks to their shop windows and spurred their mounts directly towards me, picking up speed as they came.

With just a couple of feet between them, they churned their way through the mud, thinking to knock me down or some such thing. I didn't take to the idea at all so when they got within arm's reach I grabbed both sets of reins down close to the bridle bits and yanked down and sideways.

I hated to treat animals that harshly but I did it anyway.

The result was the prettiest thing you ever did see. Those horses stopped like they had hit a wall. Their heads turned in and their rumps turned out. Their feet slipped in the mud and both fell to their sides, spilling their riders into that rain-soaked muck. It was like I was having my own private little rodeo right there in that dreary little Dakota town.

I let my hands slide down the leather until I had a longer grip on the reins and allowed the horses to scramble to their feet, holding them from running away.

Bushy Face had clearly broken a leg when his horse fell on him. His screech of pain told me he wasn't about to go anywhere any time soon. Skinny got stomped on as his horse was scrambling to its feet. That slowed him down considerably, too.

Bushy Face pulled a six-shooter from under his coat. I didn't like his intent but a quick kick from my mud-encrusted boot sent the gun flipping through the air and into the muck. I nearly lost my balance and had to stifle a groan when my weight came back down on that swollen knee.

It took but a moment or two for me to drop the saddles off the horses; dropped them right into that oozing mud and then I removed the bridles. I whapped those two brutes as hard as I could across their rumps with the bridle reins and the last I saw of them they were running free as if they were in a hurry to get to Montana and to put North Dakota behind them. Maybe they were hoping to find some sunshine.

There was a gathering of folks on the sidewalks and in the windows including the sheriff who showed no sign that he wanted to brave the rain by coming out from under the sidewalk overhang.

I reached under my oiled canvas coat and pulled my own weapon, thankful that I had taken time to clean it. I half-lifted Bushy Face and dragged him closer to his partner so I could address them both at once, him screaming in pain as I did it.

I kicked each of them in the ribs to get their attention and bent over close, pointing my Colt first into one face and then the other.

When I was sure I had their attention, I spoke for the first time, "Boys, you're thieves and who knows what else. Were we out on the prairie I'd just shoot you both and leave you for the coyotes but since we're in town with all these folks watching, I'm only going to shoot one of you. The one I'm not going to shoot is the one that tells me where my money poke is. So this is like a contest. Who's going to speak first? Where's my poke?"

Now I'm here to tell you that you never heard two such willing talkers. I guess they took me at my word and wanted desperately to be the one to stay alive.

It was nothing but a frightened and whisky-soaked jumble of sound that I had trouble making out until Bushy Face reached into a shirt pocket and pulled out my little leather sack. He passed it to me and pointed to his mate. "It was his idea right from the start. I never done noth'n like that before. You gotta believe me, mister."

Skinny started to argue but another kick in the ribs quieted him.

The rain continued to fall.

I opened the leather sack and counted the bills and gold coin. It was shy a few dollars but I wasn't one to deny a man a drink now and then so, satisfied with the count and pleased to have the most of my money back, I slid it into my coat pocket.

I leaned over Skinny, placed my muddy boot firmly on his chest, aimed my gun at his head and said, "Sorry, feller, but a deal is a deal."

As he screamed and tried to sit up, I pulled the trigger. Even over the sound of the shot I could hear a collective gasp from the crowd on the sidewalk. Mud splattered the side of Skinny's face and Bushy Face rolled desperately, trying to get away. He cried out in pain and rolled back.

I took a serious look at the man in the mud and saw there were tears welling up in his eyes. Not feeling the least bit sorry for him I said, "I missed. I never miss. It must be the rain. Hold still while I try again."

He scrunched his eyes up as if not wishing to see what was happening and reached for me with his hands.

My foot still pressing down on his chest, I took careful aim and pulled the trigger. More mud flew, coating his face and hair. This time the man managed to sit up and grab for the gun. I kicked him back down. I said, "I missed again. There must be something wrong with this gun."

By this time the sheriff had left the dry security of the sidewalk and ventured out into the mud. "Here you, that's enough. I'll not have you shooting folks right here on our main street."

Without even looking at him I said, "Don't you be a bother to me, Sheriff. I ain't in no good mood. I welcomed these men to my fire a short while back and fed them coffee. I let them share my Dakota grass, rolling out their beds beside my fire. They showed their thanks by robbing me. On top of that I've ridden and camped through three long days of rain, getting maybe four hours sleep in all that time.

"My horse slipped in the mud and I took a ride down a hill that no man nor beast should ever set out to ride down, laming my horse and myself, too, and losing my hat in the bargain.

"I had a long, five-mile walk to town leading a limping horse and all my earthly possessions are soaked. I'm standing to my ankles in your mud with your rain pounding down on my bare head and the fellers that robbed me come to do me physical harm.

"I haven't eaten in two days or had coffee for three.

"What I'm trying to tell you is that I'm just not in no good mood. I figure that shooting this thief would brighten my day some."

After a short pause, I continued, "But I might let it go if you just take him to jail. You might want to search their saddlebags, too. No telling what else they've picked up along the way."

The sheriff said, "Help me drag them in."

"I've done what-all I intend doing, Sheriff. Now I'm going to get something to eat. Drag them in or shackle them right here or cover them over with mud and call it a day. It makes no never mind to me."

3

NOAH

I REPLACED the spent shells in my Colt before putting it back in its holster.

I left the sheriff standing there in the rain, his boots sinking in the mud. I made my slow way over to the cafe, scraped my boots on the edge of the boardwalk and stepped into the eating place. The first sense of warmth I had felt in days wafted over me carrying with it the good odor of cooking and coffee which competed with the wet dog smell of wet woolen clothing and muddy boots.

A pleasant voice invited, "Sit down, mister. I'll get you coffee and whatever else you want that's available."

I turned and looked into the eyes of one of the prettiest women I'd ever seen. She wasn't really beautiful but she had an attractiveness that I figured would last through the years. Not young but not really old either, maybe in her middle twenties. The way she took charge in the cafe showed maturity and self-confidence that I liked right away.

She had left off the girlish looks of youth and taken on a fine figure that was pleasant to my thirty-year-old eyes. What I suspected was long blonde hair was tied into a roll on the back of her head.

I looked into her smiling blue eyes, my mood considerably brightening, and said, "I'll take the coffee and whatever you have to eat that's hot. But what I really need to do is have a wash. Is there a basin anywhere around that a feller might use?"

She pointed to the back door. "You'll find anything you need right out there."

I hung up my wet coat and looked to where the waitress had pointed. Several men and one woman were watching me.

I walked out onto a covered porch and found a basin hanging on a nail driven into the wall. On a small table sat a bucket of well water, a bar of lye soap and a roller towel. I lifted the basin down, scooped several dippers full of water into it and rolled up my sleeves. About that time the blonde stuck her arm out the door and passed me a dry towel. "That roller towel has seen some hard use. You might want to use this."

After a thorough scrubbing of my hands and arms, I tossed the water out into the alley and filled the basin again. The lye soap had nearly taken the skin off my hands so I washed my face and neck with plain water.

A glance in the mirror that was tacked to the wall told me that my hair and beard were beyond whatever small help was available at the time so I just toweled off the best I could, ran my fingers through the damp and tangled mop and let it go at that. I rolled down my sleeves, emptied and wiped out the basin, hung it back on the nail and re-entered the cafe.

When I got back to my table, there was coffee waiting and as soon as I sat down the blonde placed a generous bowl of beef stew in front of me along with a stack of fresh, warm bread and a mound of homemade butter. "Eat up. If you want more, just holler out."

I had finished the first bowl of stew and was starting on the second when the sheriff walked in and pulled out a chair at my table. Several other patrons stopped eating and watched us as if expecting to see a show. The sheriff sat down across from me and placed his elbows on the table, looking as if he had a mind full of questions.

"Care to join me, Sheriff?"

The man just grunted an unintelligible response. The blonde placed another cup of coffee on the table.

The sheriff sipped at the coffee and then reached over with his muddy hands to pick up a slice of my bread. His arm movements caused a trail of dried mud flecks to drop from his coat sleeve onto the table.

He folded the bread over and dipped it in his coffee, slurping the dripping mess into his mouth. He wiped his mustache with the back of his filthy hand.

"Took that one feller into the jailhouse and found a couple of men to tote the other over to the doc's place to have his leg splinted up. You did a number on those boys. On me and the town, too. It looked for all the world that you were really going to shoot that feller. Scared to death he was. They were fussing a bit about their runaway horses, too. I do believe they intend to lay that at your doorstep."

I saw no reason to respond.

"I'd like your name for my records and would appreciate the full of your story."

I finished eating my stew, ignoring him while I did it, him fidgeting and looking uncomfortable all the while. I finally pushed back my plate with a satisfied groan and looked at him. Before I could speak, the pretty blonde walked over and offered me a slice of apple pie and a wedge of cheese to top it off. Smiling at her, I said, "I can't think of anything more welcome. Thank you."

She brought the pie and the sheriff said, "I could go a slice of that myself."

The waitress gave him a stern look. "When you go out back and have a wash, and lay a dime on the table, I'll bring you some. Not before."

The sheriff bristled. "A dime's a lot of money for a slice of pie. Does Woody know how you're treating his customers while he's away? Robbery, that's what it is. I'll have a good mind to talk to Woody about this when he gets back."

"You do that, Sheriff. But in the meantime, you go take a wash and lay a dime on the table or else take your muddy boots and filthy hands out of my restaurant. I've seen you eat and walk out without paying more times than I can count with Woody ignoring it but you won't do that with me."

Someone at another table laughed. The sheriff hunched into his shoulders as if he was hurting, but he got up and went to wash and then laid a dime on the table.

In four gigantic bites, the sheriff's pie was gone. He pushed his plate back and wiped his mouth again. "I still haven't heard your name, mister, or just what you're doing here."

I didn't really feel like talking with the sheriff. What I wanted was a bath and about two days of sleep but I saw no way out.

"My name's Noah Gates. And I've heard every possible comment over the years about Noah and rain so don't start. What I'm doing here is absolutely none of your business nor is it the business of anyone else. But if it helps your digestion any, I'll tell you that I'm just passing through and as soon as the weather clears and my horse is healed up, all you'll see of me is dust going away. That is, if it ever dusts up in this country."

The sheriff wasn't really satisfied but he must have figured he had all he was going to get. He stood up and put on his hat. "Comes right to it, you didn't really do anything but put a scare into a couple of drunk thieves. Not much I can do about that but don't you go to cause me any more trouble.

"I need to examine those saddles and packs before I decide what to do with those two old boys. Do you intend to press charges on their thievery?"

I shook my head to indicate my intention. "I'll figure the broken leg and a night or two as your guest will be punishment enough since I got my property back. What you find in their packs could change all that but that has nothing to do with me. You might advise them that leaving me alone would be a good thing to do. Better for all of us."

I paid for the meal and thanked the waitress. My next stop was the hotel where I reserved and paid for a room. As the clerk was writing it up, I asked, "Anywhere around here a man can get a bath and some clothes washed?"

He pointed with his pen at the south side of the hotel. "You go down that alleyway and out back. Down beside the river there's a Chinese family offering baths and laundry. Two bits for a bath. Thirty-five cents if you want to be the first to use the water. They'll do your laundry and bring it right to your room here if you ask them to."

I thanked him and headed to the mercantile. I stepped in the door and was greeted by a rotund, bald-headed man behind the counter.

"Welcome, stranger. Quite a show you put on a while back. You sure spooked old Jamison. That's the sheriff, in case he forgot to introduce himself. I could see from way over here that he had no idea at all what to do. When you fired that shot into the mud, I come near laughing right out loud seeing Jamison jump. What can I do for you?"

"Everything I own is soaked through and covered in river mud. I need you to outfit me from the skin out, boots and hat included."

Twenty minutes later, I walked out of the mercantile with a paper-wrapped bundle of clothes and a pair of boots slung over my shoulder by their tied-together laces. I made my way to the laundry and asked about the bath. A girl I took to be about sixteen or seventeen years old pointed towards an alcove at the back.

I dropped my boots on the floor beside a large wooden barrel that had been cut down for use as a bathtub. There was a small seat fixed inside.

I placed the parcel of clothing on a small bench. The girl had followed me in. I turned to her and said, "I'd like hot clean water and a bar of soap. I'll be back in a short while."

She nodded and answered, "The water is always on the stove so you can come when you are ready. There's shaving gear on the stand over there if you're interested."

I don't know exactly what I was expecting from the Chinese girl but I was pleasantly surprised at her good grammar, a valuable skill that I admitted I was losing the longer I stayed in the West.

I left my purchases in the bathhouse and went outside. I plowed my way through the mud again and entered the livery barn. The rain was dwindling off to a sprinkle. The hostler was working over Sam so I picked up a curry comb and brush and started on Rascal. But first I pulled out a small sack of cafe leftovers the blonde had given me and laid it on the floor for Wolf.

The horses attended to, I picked up my two packs and slopped back across the street. My knee was hurting like thunder but I was never much on asking for help so I got the job done.

I dropped one pack inside the hotel door and carried the other to the laundry, limping more with each step. I pointed at the canvas pack and said to the girl, "Everything in there is soaked including the pack itself. I'd like if you could find time to run it all through the wash and bring it to Room Seven in the hotel when it's done. No particular hurry. I'm not going anywhere for a few days."

She said something in Chinese to a man I took to be her father. He came over and dragged the pannier away. She then pointed to the alcove. "Your tub is ready. If you need more hot water, just call me. Take your time. There are no other customers."

I thanked her and said, "When I get in the tub, perhaps your father can come and get these clothes, too. And maybe you can find some way to clean and dry the boots."

Nothing in this world ever felt so good as that shave and then the hot bath. I soaked until the water was cold, dried myself off with a rough towel the girl brought me, and dressed in the new clothing; boots, hat and all. I left the laundry feeling almost human, my mood somewhat lightened and wanting another cup of coffee.

The blonde welcomed me again with a smile. "Well, you look like a new man. You clean up pretty good." She said this as if we were old friends which I immediately thought might be pleasant if it were true and brought me coffee.

Later I carried my other wet pack up to room seven and spread my things out over the floor to dry. A map I carried with me was ruined and my diary where I recorded some of my travels was looking hard-used. The three books I had packed from home looked grim but would still be readable. A few other things I would take to the laundry but first I needed sleep.

I slept the late afternoon through and then the night. I needed that much sleep again but, when the morning sun woke me, I felt almost human so I dressed and went out to face the new day. The sun was shining and the street was beginning to dry up.

The same blonde was working at the cafe. When she came with coffee, I asked, "Do you work all the time?"

She showed me a tired smile. "There's only me and Mable, the cook. The owner is away for a couple of weeks so, if the door is open, Mable and I are here."

I followed the driest path I could find to the livery trying to save my new boots. I fed the dog and checked on the horses.

The livery man came out of his little office and said, "Walked that bay up and down the barn a few times. He's maybe a bit better but I'd keep him out of the mud for a few more days were he mine."

I thanked him, spent a few minutes grooming the horses, cleaned some mud off my saddle and went back to the hotel. By the time I gathered up a few more things to have laundered, it was coming on to nine in the morning. I went back for another cup of coffee, found out the blonde's name was Dora, and then talked myself into going for a nap which, in my normal life, I would never have even considered.

That became my pattern for four more days during which time the rain stayed away and a brilliant prairie sun warmed the newly growing spring grass. After the fourth day, I was anxious to put the Pembina Valley behind me. I took the bay for a short ride which he handled just fine. I decided to leave the next morning, hoping the rain was gone for a while.

4

NOAH

I HAD GOTTEN to know a few folks, at least to say hello to, so that last evening in town when the bachelors gathered for their regular evening meals, I was sharing a table with a local horse trader named Silas. Silas was a big, sloped-shouldered man, pleasant enough to talk man-talk with but he seemed to me to have a leaning towards a short fuse. I'd heard him chew out one of his wranglers over a small incident that most men would have ignored.

He probably would have been thought of as handsome by some women; a regular shave and a few new clothes would have impressed the ladies even more.

Around the supper tables in the cafe, I was included in the banter although I contributed little to it myself. After some typical cowboy teasing and chuckling which came near to getting out of control, a cowhand from a local ranch hollered across the room, "So, Silas, when are you going to pop the question to Dora? She's a fine-looking lady and a good cook. What more could a man want?"

Dora's head snapped around to look first at the cowhand and then at Silas. She had a shocked look on her face, standing there as if she was frozen to the floor.

Silas grew the reddest face I'd ever seen on a man. He said not a word, his eyes firmly fixed on the table between us. Things might have settled out if it had stopped at that point but the men were revved up from all the talk and jesting of the past few minutes. As others took up the question, Silas continued to look at the table top between us.

Dora never moved. She just stood there looking at Silas. It might have been better if she had walked away.

Silas could have said something to diffuse the situation but he didn't. He could have said, "That's between Dora and me." Or he could have said, "When I ask the question, it won't include you cow nurses butting in." Or he could have said almost anything. But he said nothing at all which was probably the worst thing he could have done.

He might even have said something lighthearted that would have saved the moment but Silas seemed to have no lightheartedness in him.

The men meant no harm but harm was done just the same. Dora stood as if waiting while Silas just sat there in silence. The whole matter lasted no more than a few seconds. But that few seconds felt like a painfully long time with the men chuckling and throwing out suggestions. As the tension grew, Silas stumbled to his feet and looked at the floor in front of Dora.

"Dora, you know how I feel about you. I'd surely like to have you for a wife."

It was not a proposal that any woman would have enjoyed receiving or the circumstances to receive it in.

Dora flipped her wiping rag over her shoulder and put

her hands on her hips. "Silas, if you can't ask me like a man without the prodding of these fools and then you look at the floor all the while, why would I want to give myself to you?"

The room fell silent.

Silas stumbled to the door like a man in a daze. He missed his grab for the door latch, his momentum nearly carrying him through the window when the door didn't open. He finally reached the sidewalk, took several steps and stopped. He stood as if in thought and then walked into the saloon, slamming the swinging doors nearly off their hinges.

The cafe cleared out as fast as the men could pay for their meals. No one made eye contact with Dora. I had nothing at stake so I stayed a few moments and finished my coffee. Putting a few extra coins on the table, I nodded at Dora and said, "Great supper. Thank you."

Dora made no response.

I sauntered along to the livery to check on my animals and take Wolf his cafe scraps.

Silas must have had only one or two drinks because a few minutes later he walked into the barn and hollered at his two wranglers who had been playing poker over a bale of hay. "You two shake yourselves out and saddle up. We're moving the herd out right now."

One of the men asked, "Where we goin', boss, and how long till we get back?"

"Going to Montana. We ain't com'n back. I'll be setting up the business over there. Shake it up; I want to put this berg behind me." If he saw me working over my horses, he chose to ignore the sight.

It didn't take but ten minutes for the three men to gather their belongings, saddle up and open the corral gates. They were soon lost to sight over the western horizon but not before I had quickly checked all their brands.

I had taken a careful look at Silas's herd on my first day in town but he might have done some trading since then and it paid to be careful. Checking brands was something I was doing without hardly even thinking about it.

Sam's limp was healed up and I judged him fit for the trail. My knee still hurt me some but I could sit a saddle alright.

I was saddling up and loading my packs the next morning when Dora came into the livery. "Have you seen Silas this morning, Mr. Gates?"

"He pulled out last evening, Dora. Him and his two wranglers and the horses. Said he was taking the business to Montana."

Looking troubled and embarrassed, she asked me, "Where are you heading, Mr. Gates? Are you going in the direction of Montana?"

"Well, Dora, Montana covers a whole lot of territory and it's a far ride from here. I'm heading generally in that direction but I have no specific goal; I'm mostly just riding around, seeing country. I'm planning to end up in the Colorado gold fields in a few weeks when the sun has had a chance to drive the snow out of the high mountain valleys.

"There's no telling what part of Montana Silas will head for. What did you have in mind?"

"I'll trust you with my thoughts, Mr. Gates, because I need help. Silas is basically a good man. He'll never be rich or refined and he'll never be comfortable in genteel surroundings but he's steady and he makes a decent living. I'm no longer young, Mr. Gates. While I'm not quite desperate, I'm also not casual about my future. I'm thinking I let the bantering in the cafe last evening get in the way of my good sense. And certainly Silas did. I'd like to find him and see if we can work it out. If you were going that way, I could pay you a bit to escort me."

I looked out over the prairie, gathered my thoughts, looked back at my half-loaded packhorse and then turned to Dora. "I don't want your money, Dora, but you could ride along west if you really want to and if you could be ready quickly. As you can see, I'm pretty much set to get under way.

"But I have to ask you, have you considered your reputation and what folks might say about you traveling alone with a man you barely know?"

Dora smiled as she turned to go. "Folks are going to think whatever they want no matter what I do. I'll guard my morals and hope that others will guard their tongues."

I thought that might be placing more faith in human nature than what was deserved but I let it go.

Dora continued, "I won't be more than a few minutes getting ready. Most of my necessaries are already packed. I'll just go get them. They don't amount to much. Perhaps there's room on your packhorse for a small satchel."

She didn't wait for my answer but continued on towards her boarding house, talking all the while.

"That's my black mare lazing around in the corral and that's my saddle with the rain slicker draped over it. If you could saddle up for me, we could be under way in just no time at all. Thank you, Mr. Gates."

"What about the cafe?" I hollered at her retreating back.

She answered without slowing her steps, "I closed it for the day. Woody is back tomorrow; he'll look after it. Anyway, this is more important."

Within a half-hour we were riding west and within an hour we had picked up the trail of a group of horses that almost had to be Silas and his bunch.

We made pretty good time on our first day of travel, all things considered. Dora's mare had been getting lazy, spending its time in the town corral and eating cut hay with only once in a while running free in the town pasture or being taken for a ride. So I had to keep slowing or stopping while Dora kicked a little more action out of the mare's unwilling hide.

But by late afternoon we had come upon a sheltering growth of aspens with just a scattering of spruce outlining the grove and a small creek of running water so we called it enough for the first day. I had no way of knowing if we were still in Dakota or had crossed into Montana. Nor did it really matter. The distances were far and the miles ahead looked just like the miles behind.

Dora had little to say during the ride and I probably had less. I figured she was mulling over what words she would use when we came up to Silas. There was no way it could be easy for a lady of genteel nature to approach a man who had made a fool of himself and her, too, in front of the group in the cafe.

I was pretty sure her mind was full of thoughts and words about her and Silas, and that anything I said would help just none at all. So we rode the long day through, eating a lunch of cafe sandwiches and creek water. By evening, Dora nearly fell off her horse, she was that tired.

She spread out her bedroll and groaned as she lay down. "I'm dead, Mr. Gates, I am absolutely dead. We should have brought a shovel so you could bury me and rid yourself of a burden. I haven't ridden a full day in nearly a year." After a short pause, she again said, "I'm dead."

I chuckled a bit and looked up from where I was putting a fire together. "You'll be alright come mornin'. I'll put on a bite to eat and you can turn in early. My guess is that you'll be up shaking the branches in the morning, waking up the birds so's they can get an early start on their day's activities."

"I strongly doubt that, Mr. Gates. In fact, you may have to go borrow a wagon to load me in or else just leave me here. Or you could find that shovel I talked about and put me out of my misery."

All was silent for a full minute when she suddenly sat up, looking startled like she'd just remembered something important. "Mr. Gates, I should have told you I don't do well in early mornings. Pa tried everything he could think of to get me going on the farm but finally gave it up. I could never understand just exactly why a cow has to be milked in the dark of a winter morning. And chickens have all day with nothing at all to do so if they get fed a bit later, what's the difference? Promise me we can at least get a decent night's sleep even if my body never recovers."

She sounded right serious about the matter so I assured her that all would be well. "You can be sure of getting a good sleep starting right after supper."

She sat there and watched me putting grub together and finally struggled to her feet. "Mr. Gates, how would it be if you care for the horses and check out this campsite for snakes while I make supper? I don't mean to be critical but watching you makes me somehow doubt the outcome of that process. Just slide that pan off the heat while I stagger down to the creek to wash. Then I'll see what can be done."

Her slow walk to the creek confirmed how she felt but she was determined so I went to the horses.

I tethered the horses on good grass where they could all reach the creek to water at their leisure. Then I stacked our saddles and gear along with my panniers under a large spruce where they might have a bit of shelter in case of rain. I covered all of that with a small ground sheet I carried with me.

I gathered more wood and stopped by the fire. "Smells good, Dora. A man on the trail mostly eats to stay alive. Taste don't have much to do with it. But I can sure sit up and take notice when something better than my own fixings comes along. I'll be sorry to lose you tomorrow."

"Tomorrow, Mr. Gates? I've seen no sign of anything or anyone except for those tracks we're following. Do you really think we will catch up by tomorrow?"

I poured myself a cup of coffee and grinned at her. "I could be tempted to slow down or even get lost for a few days, smelling that grub. You're not half-bad company either. Most women chatter about nothing all the day long but not you. I enjoyed our ride today."

Dora gave me a searching look with just a bit of a smile attached. "You have vast experience with chattering women, do you, Mr. Gates?"

Well, she had me there. We grinned at each other and I pushed my hat further back on my head so I could see her better from under the brim. "Mostly I just heard that. You know, around campfires and round-up chuck wagons. Are you suggesting that all those weather-worn, never-married, old range busters didn't know what they were talking about and filling a young sprout's mind with nonsense?"

"I expect each man speaks from his own experience or viewpoint."

It baffled me how Dora managed to put together a feeding such as what she laid before me from the bit of fixings I had in my packs. It was good and I told her so.

She scrubbed up the dishes while I kicked through the grass looking for varmints and then I laid out my bedroll. I placed it close enough to still be in the same camp but far enough away to give Dora some comfort and privacy.

Dora fidgeted around a bit until I finally woke up to her needs. I looked and felt kind of sheepish and finally said, "It's time I took a look further out from camp, see where best to head in the morning. I won't be far away so you can just holler if something troubles you."

Understanding my meaning, she blushed the prettiest pink blush and nodded. I could barely hear her whispered, "Thank you."

I scouted all around within a quarter mile or so and saw nothing to concern me. When I returned to the campsite, Dora was sound asleep, snoring lightly. She had turned her bedroll so she was facing the fire from maybe twenty feet away. She had the bedroll pulled up right over her head, probably to block out the evening sun. I figured she was gone till morning and I had a long evening ahead of me sitting alone.

I let my mind drift for a few moments, thinking about opportunities lost and chances not taken; chances that might have led to a wife and a home instead of all this single wandering. There'd been a girl back yonder. I couldn't remember the name of the town. She had seemed to be a girl who had staying power and one who could think on her own. Pretty, too. Just what she saw in me I couldn't exactly say. No doubt there was opportunity to settle down and work on getting to know her. Still, I saddled up and rode out after a quick goodbye. I didn't have an answer when she asked where I was going and why. She gave me a sad, pitying look and watched me swing into the saddle.

"Goodbye, Noah," was all she said as I swung my horse toward the open prairie. I still don't know exactly why I left.

Like every far-riding man, I was familiar with long evenings alone and accepted them as just another part of my chosen life.

When I woke in the morning, the first thing I did after stepping into my pants and pulling on my shirt was reach for my hat. When that was done, I was pretty much ready for the day. Then I brought the horses in. Wolf had spent the night beside the horses so I hadn't worried about them. I tied them to aspen trees and threw their saddles on. Then I started breaking sticks for kindling, figuring the noise would wake Dora but no such a thing happened. I ignored her for a few minutes while the fire caught hold and then I put the coffeepot on.

Dora looked like she hadn't moved through the whole long night. I finally called over to her, "Wake up, Dora. The day's a wasting."

After saying it a second time, a hand rose from the bedding and waved me off as if telling me to be quiet. That movement was accompanied by a mumbled, "Mmfft."

Chuckling to myself, I picked up a larger piece of wood and broke it over my knee purposely making noise and then I did it twice more. The hand rose from the bedding again, pointing a pistol in my general direction although Dora still hadn't moved her head.

There was barely enough light to see but there was no doubt about what was in her hand. The pistol waved around some and again I was all set to chuckle to myself when she pulled the trigger and blew the coffeepot right off the fire, spilling coffee and burning wood in every direction.

I dove behind a small grassy knoll and was about to shout out when Dora leaped from her bed. Now she was wide awake and terrified at what she had done. "Mr. Gates, Mr. Gates, where are you? Are you alright? Oh, my goodness, what have I done? Mr. Gates, are you there?" She was waving the pistol around the whole time.

I raised my head just a bit. "Put the gun down, Dora. Put it down."

She didn't seem to know that she was still carrying it. Finally, she looked at her right hand, let out another startled yelp, and dropped the gun on the ground. I slowly got to my knees and then to my feet. Dora cried out, "Are you alright, Mr. Gates?" and took a step towards me. She placed her foot down on a root or a sharp rock, I couldn't see which. She cried out in pain and started jumping on one foot.

I didn't much feel like smiling but I did it anyway. "I'm alright. I'm glad you aren't a better shot or you might have had to get that shovel for me."

"I'm actually a very good shot when I'm awake. Please forgive me. I started carrying the pistol on my ride west last year. I am absolutely terrified of snakes. And I'm not really on good speaking terms with spiders either. The pistol seemed like a good idea at the time. I had no intention of shooting you. I told you I don't do well in the early morning but I had no...," then she noticed the coffeepot. "Did I do that? Oh, Mr. Gates, whatever must you think of me?"

"Well," I answered her, "I think I will keep your pistol in my saddlebag from now on and, also, I think you look very fetching in whatever it is you're wearing. But if we're going to ride, perhaps you should get dressed."

It was only then that Dora realized she was in her flannel nightgown, standing there before me. She tried to cover herself with her hands but finally gave it up and turned to her clothing hanging from a low aspen branch.

She took two steps and then, as if thinking some new startling thought, she whirled towards me demanding,

"What are you doing up, Mr. Gates? And why did you wake me? It's still dark as a coal mine. I thought we were going to get a good night's sleep. If this is your idea of morning, we are going to have to disagree on that definition. Perhaps you should ride on by yourself, Mr. Gates, if you insist on calling night day and dark light. Why I can't understand...,"

My laugh stopped her talking. "I liked it better, Dora, when you went the whole of a day without chattering. I thought you wanted to catch up to Silas. For sure he'll be up and boiling coffee by now and we won't catch him lying in our bedrolls. Anyway, by the time we eat, there'll be pink in the east and full sunrise not long after."

I'm not sure if Dora was talking to me or to herself or just mumbling but she turned again to her tree-hung clothing and I heard words like, 'Pink in the east, oh good!' and 'No time at all till full sunrise!' and 'What have I gotten myself into?'

I chuckled again and went for a short walk to give her more privacy while she dressed. We were soon under way with Dora having finally gotten herself ready, splashing cold creek water on her face after which she fried up some bacon and then the four eggs I had carefully wrapped before leaving town.

I filled the coffeepot from the creek and put it on the rebuilt fire. The bullet holes allowed for about a half a pot of coffee so we settled for that although we both longed for another cup. Nothing more was said about the pistol or the shooting but the pistol was safely tucked away in my saddlebag.

5

NOAH

WE MADE good time and the dew-wet, hoof-churned grass made the tracking easy. We camped in a copse of aspens beside a slow-flowing creek the next night and caught up to Silas at noon on our third day. We were watched into their noon camp but we stopped at a respectable distance anyway.

"Hello the camp. How's about some coffee and a word or two?"

Silas stood with his hands on his hips for a full minute before he walked out to where we were still sitting our saddles. He didn't invite us to get down or join the fire or have coffee. "What are you two doing out here?"

I spurred my horses a short ways away to give them a bit of privacy.

Dora was pretty taken back by his coolness but she stumbled ahead with her plan. "Can we sit and talk for a few minutes, Silas?"

Silas had a strange look about him as a man with deeply hurt pride might have. I could see his wanting when he looked at Dora but his belligerence got the better of him. "I don't see as how we have anything to talk about."

Again, Dora was forced to carry on the conversation. "Silas, we walked out together a few times and took some buggy rides. I regret the incident in the cafe the other evening and I was thinking you might regret it, too. I asked Mr. Gates to escort me so I could try to find you and maybe put that incident behind us and start again. Are you telling me that you have no desire in that direction?"

Silas showed no bend at all; prideful or stubborn, or perhaps a bit of both. "I suppose I might have had some desire that way but, now, what kind of a woman would travel across country with a strange man, doing what-all we'll never know? Why I'd be the laughingstock of the territory. Best you two be on your way. It's also best if we never see each other again."

"What are you suggesting, Silas? Are you suggesting that Mr. Gates and I...?"

Again, Silas had just no bend in him at all. "What I'm suggesting is that no decent woman would travel across country with a stranger and expect to be believed. I think you should ride on. I've got no more to say to either one of you."

Dora stared at him, unbelief showing on her face. Then she burst into tears, hiding her face in her hands. I suspect that the tears were more over his hurtful words than his rejection of her offer to reconcile.

I stepped off my horse, ground-hitched him with dropped reins, hung my brand-new Stetson on the saddle horn, and slowly walked over to Silas.

"You're a sad piece of work, Silas." Then I hit him just as hard as I could, my big fist landing on his mouth and nose.

I'm a big man and although I prefer to live in peace, the few occasions where I had hit someone in times past they had for sure known they were hit.

My fist came away with a tooth stuck in my knuckle. I yanked the tooth out while I watched blood literally flood from his nose, soaking into his flannel shirt. He looked surprised and cross-eyed so I hit him again, same place. This time he went to the ground, his arms flailing as he went over backwards.

I was sorely tempted to put the boots to him but, instead, I stepped back and watched as he struggled to get to his feet. "Get up, you useless piece of trash and take what's coming to you."

On one knee and one foot he squatted there, shaking his head, the blood still dripping from his broken nose and smashed lips.

A shout from Dora warned me. I spun on my heel in time to see the two wranglers running towards me with their guns drawn. A couple of wild shots sailed over my head, putting Dora and me both in danger.

I had never seen any good results from delaying things so I pulled my own Colt and drove several shots into the ground at their feet. You never saw two men stop so fast. I warned them, "You put those guns away and forget it. My next shot will be for keeps."

Silas used the time to stagger to his feet. I holstered my Colt and turned. I was just in time to run into a brick wall that turned out to be Silas's fist. The punch raised a welt on my cheek and rang bells in my head.

He got a short thrust into my belly and was set to try to finish me off when I finally got my balance. My sore knee wailed out an objection but I managed to stand and plant my good leg firmly on the prairie sod.

Silas tried for my belly again but my big belt buckle

took the worst of it. He withdrew a damaged hand and glanced at his bleeding knuckles.

We went toe-to-toe then, neither man backing up for long and both losing a shirt in the process. Neither of us showed any style or grace or knowledge of boxing. We were just two big men settling a difference in the only way we knew.

Dora sat her horse with her hands to her mouth as if she had never seen such horror. The two wranglers stood a little further off and stayed out of it.

It was more luck than good planning but I finally landed a looping right where my first punch had landed: on Silas's nose and bleeding mouth. I saw his eyes roll back in his head and I could see that all the fight was draining out of him.

Silas went down and stayed down.

I backed up and dropped my hands to my sides.

Neither of us looked fully human at that point and it occurred to me what a big problem can arise out of such a little thing; just an off-chance remark in a cafe and a man's hurt pride.

Looking at Silas and somewhat understanding the pride of a man, I might have felt sorry for him. But I have little compassion for a fool and none at all for a man who will down-put a lady.

I pulled a few shreds of my ruined shirt off my arm and nudged Silas with the toe of my boot. His groan told me he was conscious.

I had trouble finding the breath to talk but I managed to mumble, "Silas, you're a tough man but not much of a man in spite of your toughness. This good woman came out here to talk to you with her morals intact, ready to give you more of a chance than you deserve. She's too good for you. I'll see that she gets safely to another settlement.

"I doubt as how there's anything left for the two of you to talk about so don't you decide to follow. And if I ever hear that you've been bothering her, I'll come find you and we'll go around and around again."

I wasn't at all sure that I wanted to go around and around again with Silas but the words were said before I got a chance to think it through.

"We're heading to Miles City. I don't want to see you there. You'd best continue on west."

I wiped some blood off the back of my hand onto Silas's shirt and struggled into the saddle, my knee screaming in pain. I led off to the southwest and Dora followed saying nothing, her head hanging and, I think, her eyes closed.

I was hurting. The pain of the fight seemed to course through every part of me. And the longer we rode the worse I hurt. My knee felt like I must have twisted it again during the fight. I pulled my foot from the stirrup and let the leg hang loose.

A couple of miles further along, we splashed through a small, running stream. Dora broke the strained silence.

"Pull up here, Mr. Gates."

It wasn't a suggestion.

By the time I had sorted out her few words, she was off her horse and giving me a bleak stare.

"We need to get you cleaned up a bit."

I came near to collapsing when my weight hit that wrenched knee. I hung on to the saddle horn until I got my balance. I waited a moment for my head to clear and then hobbled to the creek. I felt the need for a drink so I half-knelt, half-fell by the stream and scooped water into my hand and up to my damaged mouth.

I rinsed my mouth out with several scoops of water. I spat bloody froth and rinsed some more until I finally felt half human.

I pulled off the remains of my shirt and buried my head in the stream. I washed my hair and scrubbed the blood and dirt off my face and hands. I squatted back on my haunches and let the water drip off me.

Dora picked up the remains of my shirt and started wiping my hair and face dry. She used one finger under my chin to tip my face towards her. My vision was a bit blurred but I think I saw her wince.

"Oh, Mr. Gates, would you just look at this eye. It's already starting to swell and blue up and I fear it's going to get worse before it gets better. And your cheek is cut. But the eye is the worst. It's going to turn swollen and black and take just forever to heal. I surely hope no one thinks I did this to you.

"Oh, that sounds awful, doesn't it? Here you are hurting and I'm worrying about what someone might think of me."

She dabbed and wiped some more. I finally pushed her hands away. I took the torn shirt from her, dried my arms and hair a bit, and threw the shirt behind a creek-side bush.

It would have been too much effort to answer her so I got slowly to my feet, limped over to my packhorse and dug another shirt from a pannier. I pulled the shirt on and let it hang outside my pants. To tuck it in would have required strength I wasn't sure I possessed.

I took a firm grip on the horn and somehow managed to get back into the saddle. I spurred forward because that was all I knew to do. There was nothing behind us that I wanted and nothing where we stood. That left forward as the only choice. If Dora decided to follow, she was welcome.

I heard nothing for a short while and then Wolf barked. He had taken to walking beside Dora's horse, showing little appreciation for my care over the months. The closeness of the dog's bark told me Dora was following along. She was soon riding beside me like she had been doing the past couple of days.

Neither of us spoke again until Dora said, "You're a bit sudden, Mr. Gates. Thinking it over, I realize that there was no chance for a future with Silas but still, I must say, you're a bit sudden.

"It's true that Silas was cruelly mean and I am sure you were protecting my honor, and perhaps some of your own as well, but I wish there had been another way to accomplish that."

I kind of slumped back in the saddle, my emotions settling down. I never ran from a fight but I can't say I enjoyed them either. But the fact is, I could sometimes get right worked up over a disagreement where others might take it in their stride. In situations like that, there was no telling what might happen.

When I was pretty sure I could speak in a normal voice, I glanced at Dora.

"I have a lot of shortcomings, Dora, but I can't abide a man foul-mouthing a lady. And while we're talking about it, I think you need to drop the Mr. Gates thing. My name is Noah. You're welcome to use it, same as everyone else. It looks as if we might be together for a while yet so let's get past the name thing."

The talking hurt my lips and the inside of my mouth.

"Thank you for that trust and for your protection, Mr. Gates, but I'll continue to call you by your full name...for now anyway."

6

DORA

I DON'T KNOW what shocked me most; Silas and his foul suspicions of me or Mr. Gates and his readiness to use force to solve any problem that confronted him. Still, I would have to admit that when Mr. Gates dealt with something, it was well and truly dealt with whether it was the thieves lying in the muddy road in town or Silas bleeding from his pulverized mouth and nose.

None of his solutions would have been seen as civilized in an eastern city. But sparsely settled Dakota and Montana were a long way from any eastern city or any effective law enforcement for that matter. I was coming to understand that the ways of Mr. Gates were very western ways. It seems that if a dispute is between two equal men, it is seen in the west as a fair fight and no one interferes.

We rode for a couple of hours and then stopped to rest and water the horses. Neither of us had anything more to say so we sat there in the prairie sunshine thinking our own thoughts.

Finally Mr. Gates wordlessly stepped back into his saddle and moved off towards the southwest. I followed along with the dog staying close by me.

Mr. Gates seemed to be just a bit out of sorts, something beyond the matter of the fight as if he was puzzling out some problem. I kept quiet, my mind deep in my own troubles.

After maybe a quarter-hour had passed, he spoke, "Well, Dora, where do you have in mind to go now? We're three full days' ride back to the cafe and I have no real idea how far from anything around these parts. But I'll take you wherever you wish to go.

"I expect the gold hills will have the snow off them pretty soon now so I'd prefer if you wished to keep going south."

I felt a terrible guilt for what I had put upon Mr. Gates, him taking on the responsibility of my escort and then for the unpleasantness with Silas.

To be outright rejected by a man such as Silas and on such foolish grounds was almost more than I could bear.

I had probably cost Mr. Gates a full day or more traveling further to the west than he had planned, on top of the troubles. I had been trying to cover my torn emotions but my voice gave me away. I wiped my eyes with the back of my hand and looked off to the west, hoping Mr. Gates hadn't seen.

"Mr. Gates, I am so terribly sorry for this mess I've gotten you into." My words came out as a series of croaks.

Mr. Gates' speech was a bit slurred, bothered by a swelling lip and - judging by the blood he kept spitting out - cuts inside his mouth.

"There's been lots worse messes, Dora, and I expect life

isn't finished throwing messes your way or mine, either one yet. Don't you be worrying about the little things."

His words had no real impact on me. I scarcely heard them. I was loaded down with guilt and sadness and maybe feeling just a little bit sorry for myself.

I was a woman alone no longer in the sweet bloom of youth, with no friends or family close by and with absolutely nothing ahead of me but single loneliness as far as my tear-filled eyes could see.

"I've cost you time, Mr. Gates, and been responsible for that unpleasantness with Silas, burdened you down like a silly helpless girl and taken you far off your original plan."

Oh, I was feeling the blue miseries all right.

Mr. Gates gave out a hearty laugh or as hearty as he could with half of his mouth swelling up. I had heard him do little more than chuckle from time to time over the days so the laugh was encouraging.

"You're all worked up over the little things, Dora. A day or two more of riding won't hurt the horses or me. We'll just keep going in the direction of the Colorado gold fields and you can stop when you see a likely place. I can wait a day or two longer before I become rich sacking up that gold."

His kind words had no effect on me at all right at that time. Here he had been through that awful fight and all I could think about was myself.

I took a couple of gulping breaths trying to stifle my sobs and then blubbered out, "And I shot your coffeepot."

Mr. Gates laughed so hard that I finally had to join him. I was laughing and crying and sniffling all at the same time; I was really a mess of self-pity and sadness.

Mr. Gates slowed his laughing long enough to say, "Indians, they rename people as they come to maturity. Name them after things they've done like 'buffalo hunter', 'steals the horses' and such. The chief would think it great sport to rename you 'shoots the coffeepot'.

Again Mr. Gates was rolling with laughter.

Although I was still blubbering, I again mixed the blubbering with a bit of laughter. Mr. Gates' cheerful strength was becoming a tonic for me and I was soon wiping my eyes and thinking more clearly.

I rode along silently for a while thinking of home and of all that had gone on there. I shared some of the remembrances with Mr. Gates.

"My father always said that I was the strong one in the family. He meant it kindly but it became a burden to me. After Dad died, it all came to rest on my shoulders and somehow I got everything done that needed doing. But I guess with getting older, and the cafe, and Silas, and all of that, I just got tired of being strong. Please forgive my momentary weakness. I'll be alright from now on.

"I have no desire at all to go back to that cafe so I might just as well ride on, if that doesn't inconvenience you too much. You can unburden yourself of me at the next town."

Mr. Gates said nothing. He simply nodded and, when he turned my way, it seemed that his lips were even more swollen than they had been before. I couldn't imagine how much he hurt.

We didn't even really discuss where we were going. I'm not sure either of us knew. Mr. Gates simply headed southwest and I followed. I certainly had no reason to go back to Dakota.

I had heard talk of several settlements off to the west that might show promise although I had no clear idea just where they were or even what they were called. Any one of them had to be as good as where I had been the past few months.

I had heard of Miles City but knew nothing at all about it or where it was except for a general direction.

Our following days of travel were mostly quiet. Mr. Gates seemed to like it that way and so did I. We rode through the untouched grass side by side, me looking at the horizon ahead or off to the west where everyone seemed to eventually end up. Mr. Gates periodically took a long look at our back trail.

I knew he was still hurting but he never complained so I said nothing. His eye was swollen almost shut and the surrounding skin was turning an alarming green color. The cut on his cheek was scabbing over and, judging by his speech, the inside of his mouth was healing.

From time to time, we saw small bunches of cattle and it seemed an infinite number of antelope.

Once we saw an old battle-scarred buffalo bull hunkered down in a rocky draw where the grass was kept green by a slow-flowing trickle of water. We pulled up and watched him for a few minutes. I tried to imagine millions of the beasts running free on all this grass but my mind wouldn't quite paint the picture.

In all of this vast land we saw not a single set of ranch buildings or even a homesteader's shack.

At our third camp after leaving Silas behind, I had washed up the dishes and cooking pot and Mr. Gates had settled down, leaning lazily against a large aspen tree, one of hundreds in the bend of a small stream. He took a sip from his last cup of coffee and looked over at me.

"Seems a long ways from anywhere for a young lady to find herself at, Dora. Do you mind if I ask what you're doing out here? Before the Silas thing I mean. It's not hard to tell that you come from a quality background. You don't hardly seem the type to be wandering the countryside."

I took some time thinking of an answer and finally admitted, "I didn't start out to wander, Mr. Gates.

"I have two brothers. We were raised on a farm in Ohio but neither of my brothers wanted to farm. They both went off to the city and found work that suited their hands better than plow handles, horse harness and barn shovels.

"I loved the farm and stayed on with the folks, working in town during the winter months either at the general store or the town newspaper.

"My mother died a few years ago. Dad and I farmed and looked after each other until he came down with pneumonia last winter. I buried him in the farm plot beside Mom."

Mr. Gates showed his understanding. "It's tough losing your folks."

I nodded in agreement and finished my story.

"I couldn't run the farm myself so I sold out. Dad kept his land in good shape and his livestock were well cared for so I had no trouble selling.

"I split the funds from the sale with my brothers with them giving back a portion to make up for my years of work after they moved to the city.

"I visited an uncle and aunt in Minnesota, hoping they would invite me to stay for a while but, after a week, it was obvious they did not wish to share either their house or their lives with me.

"I bought a horse and saddle and joined a group heading west.

"That was eight months ago. I lived through the Dakota winter waiting tables in that cafe you found me in and here I am."

We sat in silence for a while watching the small fire turn to gray ash. We both seemed to be content with the silence but finally I worked up the courage to ask, "What's your story, Mr. Gates?"

He took longer thinking of what to say than I had but he finally laid out the bare essentials.

"I love horses. They can be ornery and contrary and sometimes unpredictable but I love them just as they are. I kicked around some like most young fellows after leaving home, riding herd on other men's cattle and eating enough dust to plant a garden in. But I saved my money, most of it anyway, and bought the livery stable in this little town. That was back in Oklahoma Territory. I bought me a herd of fair-to-middling riding stock and worked up a pretty good business, trading mounts with passing trail drovers. Looking at those corralled horses, all carrying my G-bar brand, filled me with pride. Now I know what the Book says about pride but I didn't really credit the warning to myself. My fall came later.

"I bought a freight wagon and a team of matched blacks. Beautiful giants they were; feet as big as pie plates. I believe they could have pulled the moon out of the sky if I could have taken a hitch around it, but gentle as lambs. I loved those big boys."

I smiled at Mr. Gates, remembering. "Dad had a team like that. I sometimes thought he saw them as people, he loved them so."

After another short silence, Mr. Gates continued, "Just as the business was showing promise and I had made the last payment on a bank loan, someone helped himself to those horses.

"If I'd still been sleeping on the bunk in the livery office I would have heard them and been able to put a stop to the theft. But I had foolishly moved into the boarding house down the street a ways and was comfortably dreaming my life away under a feather quilt when someone opened the corral gate and drove that team and all my trade animals away in the night.

"Well, come morning I was some angry, threatening to find and hang the thieves. I saddled a horse that had been safe in the barn and set out to do justice.

"You can't hide that many horse tracks so the following of them presented no challenge. They were driving the poor beasts hard and fast and, within a short ways, I found my big blacks standing in some roadside shade - their sides heaving and their heads hanging - unable to go further. The fools that drove them off had pushed them along with the riding stock and they just weren't up to it. Those boys were made for pulling not running.

"I walked them to a small ranch a mile or so away and put them up in the barn with plenty of care that I paid the rancher's kids for. Then I took off after the herd. But by this time, they were miles away and my own horse was showing need of rest.

"The long and short of it is that I didn't find the horses.

"When I put the whole thing before the sheriff in a small town along the way, he wasn't too encouraging. He leaned back in his swivel chair with his thumbs locked behind his wide leather belt and gave me a hopeless look.

"All he had to offer was, 'I don't know what a posse could do that you haven't already done but I'll get a message out over the wire, let the other sheriffs around know. You never can tell, something may come up.'

"I never heard from the man again and don't expect to. I've been looking for G-bar horses ever since but it's unlikely after all this time that I'll ever see them again. It took me some time to get past feeling angry at myself for my carelessness and at the thieves.

"I still had the team of blacks and the freight wagon so it wasn't a total loss."

I found myself with nothing to say. After a few moments, I reached over and lay my hand lightly on Mr. Gates' wrist and gave him what I hoped was a sympathetic look.

Then, embarrassed, I quickly pulled my hand back and rose to my feet. This time, I was the first to spur off to the southwest.

7

NOAH

DORA CLIMBED aboard the saddle and kicked her horse into motion. I sat for a minute or so as she grew smaller in the distance. Wolf trotted at her side.

It took me a moment to realize that I had settled my hand on my wrist right where she had touched it. I quickly lifted it off.

My body hurt so bad I had no desire to move. I could have gladly just laid back and gone to sleep. But Dora was getting smaller in the distance. Finally, I roused myself and followed after.

Hearing Dora's story and telling some of mine got me thinking about my decisions and how I had come to be here.

After giving up on chasing the thieves, I had been an unhappy man having to admit that my G-bar horses were gone for good. I kind of lost interest in the horse-trading business and went full time to hauling freight for a while plus renting out some barn space from time to time.

Then a feller came to town with his pockets bulging with cash money. He made me an offer on the team and wagon along with the barn and corrals.

I looked at those gold coins and then over at the blacks and went for a drink while I thought it over. I'm not really a drinking man but once in a while I'll take a glass or two. There was quite a tussle in my mind for the first two drinks but with the third glass the gold won the day.

I saddled this Sam horse I'm still riding, loaded up the other one with all my worldly possessions which don't amount to much, and set out with no particular goal in mind.

A small part of me was still kind of hoping to run into my G-bar horses but, in a country as big as this, I knew the chances were slim. My anger at the thieves was a long time in settling out and maybe it isn't quite settled out yet.

Right at the end there after I swung into the saddle, I looked over at those blacks. They stood with their heads hanging over the corral fence, watching me. They had served me well and I was a guilty-feeling man riding away. But I rode away just the same. It seemed like riding away was becoming a habit.

I didn't have much to show for all my hard work and not even anyone to say good-bye to that really mattered.

I wandered kind of aimlessly from town to village, checking horse brands as I went along until I found myself riding into Deadwood with snow piling up on my hat and shoulders. It was too cold to ride any further so I stayed for the winter, managing to make expenses doing odd jobs.

But one winter in Deadwood should be enough for any thinking man. I made up my mind to move on as soon as the snow was off the trails.

Wolf took up with me in Deadwood. He seemed to have taken a liking to me from the first time I fed him one bitterly cold winter day. He was half-starved and alone, scrounging for whatever he could find on the back streets of that bleak town.

We took each other in; two creatures alone in the winter cold. I fed him and he kept me company in a drafty, poorly-built shack stuck down on the end of a crooked mountainside road. He's been traveling with me ever since.

By late winter with full spring still a distance away, I had caught a small case of gold fever listening to all the talk around. The Colorado gold fields sounded more to my liking than the Deadwood hills so that's where I'm headed for.

Of course, those high up mountains are cold country, too, but I don't figure to be there when the snow starts to fall again.

Dora was still well ahead of me so I kicked a bit more speed out of Sam and we soon caught up. We rode along side by side, content again with our silence.

As we continued our ride south and west, I thought of the Missouri River. I hadn't mentioned the river to Dora. Coming in from the east I doubted that she had even seen it. But as we rose over the crest of a hill, it lay right there before us, wide and wandering and formidable. From where we sat our horses, it looked impossible to cross. But cross it we must.

I remembered somewhat bitterly my experience riding north just a few weeks before. I foolishly took the advice of a livery man over around Bismarck.

I had waded my horses into that cold, spring run-off water where that livery man had told me there was a decent fording spot and right away found myself sitting atop a terrified horse whose feet had nothing beneath it but bone-chilling water.

I swung off my saddle and, holding the horn, did my best to encourage the animal to swim to the other side, praying he was a better swimmer than I was.

Wolf and my packhorse followed along with the rushing water carrying us all downstream. We must have traveled more than a mile before Sam's feet again touched ground.

As he started to rise out of the water, I held a frantic grip on the horn and struggled onto the saddle not at all sure my cold, stiff legs would carry me ashore if I separated from the horse.

Sam stepped up the grassy bank and stopped on the level ground beyond. I slid off his back holding one rein and fell to the ground exhausted and shivering with cold. A quick glance told me the packhorse was still at the end of his lead rope. Both horses had dropped their heads to crop the early spring grass. Wolf was shaking the cold river from his long, winter coat.

I lay soaking wet on that grass until the weak spring sun beat a bit of warmth into my bones. I found myself wondering why I had crossed the river and wishing I could get my hands on that livery man. I had no business on either side of the Missouri, come to that. I could have just as easily turned back south with nothing lost.

It took me two days with my goods spread around several shrubs to get everything dry and ready to move on.

It seems now, looking back over the weeks, that I had been wet for most of my time in North Dakota.

Now the wide Missouri lay between Dora and her new start in life and between me and the Colorado gold fields. As formidable as that expanse of water looked, neither of us had any intention of not continuing south and west.

There were places where travelers had forded the Missouri but I had no idea where they were. I wasn't about to ask another livery man either.

Dora pointed to her right. "There's a small settlement over there. Why don't we see if we can get a meal and a bath and something softer than rocky ground to sleep on for one night?"

I saw no need to answer. I simply kicked my horse into a slow walk down the slope and headed to the settlement. The name hand-painted on a broken board and nailed to a leaning-over picket fence at the edge of town said, 'Williston, pop 300.'

I looked at the sign and said to Dora, "We've been talking about how we were in Montana but I do believe Williston is in Dakota. Not that it makes any real difference to either you or me. But we could be stepping on someone's pride of home if we were to get it wrong."

8

DORA

WE HAD BEEN RIDING southwest for nearly two weeks, taking our time and seeing the country and staying within my ability to sit a saddle. Although my body eventually accepted the worst of the punishment of the saddle and sleeping on the ground, I still had limitations. I was thankful that Mr. Gates recognized those limitations without making a fuss about it.

Except for the disappointment of my meeting with Silas and all that was involved in that foolishness, the trip had been memorably enjoyable. Mr. Gates had proven to be a gentleman and good company. He had kept the camps free of snakes and we hadn't been poisoned by my camp-fire cooking. Mr. Gates had shown himself to be wary of any passing strangers, keeping his hand close to his Colt as we neared other riders. After one particularly troubling meeting with two scraggly bearded men, Mr. Gates gave me back my pistol. "Keep it handy and don't be afraid to use it. Just don't take it to bed with you."

I learned some things I hadn't realized about human nature and the dangers that presented themselves on the frontier. But all in all, the trip had been a fun adventure.

The little village of Williston didn't offer much but we did get a couple of meals and some trail supplies from the small general store including a new coffeepot that I purchased and presented to Mr. Gates. We smiled at each other as I passed it to him, enjoying our private remembrance.

The four-room hotel offered a wood stave tub in a back room for bathing which I used first thing. They had one vacant room with a rope-slung bed and a grass-filled mattress which wouldn't have looked like much in a big city hotel but looked like heaven to me. Mr. Gates waited until after dark before filling the tub with bath water for himself. He then slept in the loft at the livery barn and seemed happy enough in the morning.

Our inquiry about a low-water fording spot on the river brought a smiling response from the hotel man.

"This ol' river don't like to show the world the same face day by day. Where there's a sandbar today there might be a twenty-foot-deep hole tomorrow. Unpredictable, she is.

"Whatever low-water crossing might have been available is gone now with the upcountry snow melt. You cross on horseback, you're going to get wet. But Tyler, him that lives just upstream a ways and grows garden truck for sale in town, has a flat-bottom scow. Big old thing. Takes one man and one horse at a time. He'll pole you across.

"Cost you some for the trip but you'll arrive dry-footed and ready to get on your way."

We found the man named Tyler. He was just snubbing his scow to the landing post when we rode up. Mr. Gates lifted his Stetson a bit and addressed the boatman.

"Morning. I assume you to be Mr. Tyler."

At the man's assurance that this was so, Mr. Gates continued, "The lady and I need to get to the other side. We'd prefer to do it dry."

Tyler leaned over and spat an awful looking brown wad into the river grass. He looked over at me and the animals.

"Take three trips for the lot of you and not a one of them easy. River's near flood. Lots of sawyers and flotsam. Cost you twelve dollars for the bunch, dog included, assuming he don't cause no trouble. You or your horse falls off, you're on your own, just so's we understand."

Mr. Gates gave me a quick look but made the decision himself.

"Mr. Tyler, I swam this river a few weeks ago; me and the horses and the dog. Didn't enjoy even one minute of the crossing. If you can start now and get us there dry, I'll make it an even fifteen."

Tyler spat again. "Which of you wants to be first?"

It was decided that I would go first along with Wolf and my horse. Tyler lowered the end transom on the scow, the rusted hinges squealing in protest, and led the horse on. With a nod of his head, he directed me to the front of the wooden vessel and said, "Hold the horse. He decides to get out and walk, let him go. Don't you be following him into the water. Be the last we ever see of you."

With those few directions, he pushed off. It was only then that I saw the rope running from the scow to the shore and a young boy sitting bareback on a harnessed horse. The towline ran from the scow to the horse with a long length of rope coiled neatly in the grass. When Tyler pushed out into the water, the boy slid off the horse and ran to feed the rope off the coiled pile to keep it from tangling.

Tyler poled into the current and with a long sweep-oar directed the boat towards the south bank, the river current doing all the work. I saw the boat taking on water through the ill-fitting transom. The boards Mr. Tyler had fastened together to create the transom that became a loading ramp fit poorly, allowing the river to enter the craft at an alarming rate. As the water rose up my horse's legs, I found myself hoping we would reach land before the water filled the boat. I stepped up on a bench nailed to the side of the craft to keep my feet dry.

"Mr. Tyler," I said, "do you not worry about the water coming in the boat?"

He chuckled and grinned at me. "Don't you be worrying, young Miss. When I get back to the other side, I pull it up the sloping bank and the water all drains out. I've never sunk 'er yet."

I didn't altogether accept his assurances but we were well out into the river by that time so I braced my feet and hung onto the horse and studied the river, praying for a safe arrival at the distant bank.

The horse trembled a bit with the movement of the boat but my soft words in his ear and my grip on the bridle seemed to reassure him.

When it was far too late to turn back, I noticed a huge tree rolling over and over in the water, its roots still attached and its limbs at least thirty-feet across. I couldn't see any way for Mr. Tyler to avoid hitting the floating menace.

I probably should have held my tongue but the words were out before I thought, "Mr. Tyler…," I might have screamed the words, I'm not exactly sure.

I thought Mr. Tyler sounded a bit frightened, too. "I see it. Just hold yourself and the animal steady."

He struggled to turn the small craft upstream, slowing the boat. "Hang on, this is going to be close."

As we came near, the current spun the tree completely around. We missed the largest part of the menace but the top branches swung around and slashed their way across the boat. Wolf, standing on the seat near the front, was knocked flat into the gathered water on the bottom of the boat. I took a firm grip on the bridle and talked to the horse while the lighter top branches whipped across his head and side. I was kept safe ducked down behind the animal's head and neck. The horse threatened to make a fuss but my firm grip discouraged him and he settled down.

I turned around just in time to see a very wet Mr. Tyler picking himself up off the bottom of the boat. He pulled his hat out of the water, shook it and placed it back on his head. He picked up his oar and carried on as if nothing had happened.

In no time at all we nosed into the muddy south bank of the Missouri. Tyler got out and lowered the end ramp and we stepped ashore. I was amazed at how simple it had been. If it hadn't been for the floating tree, it would have been an enjoyable experience.

I thanked Mr. Tyler and he pushed off again, signaling with his raised hat for the boy on the horse to pull him back. In less than an hour Mr. Tyler had Noah and his two horses standing dry on the south bank.

I had built a fire while I was waiting for Noah and when the packhorse arrived, I put together some lunch. Within two hours we were on our way south again, this time following the Yellowstone River.

Riding away from the Missouri, Mr. Gates told me the

details about his crossing just a few weeks before. I chuckled at the story and Mr. Gates joined me with a strained smile.

We followed the Yellowstone as it wound its crooked way towards the far distant mountains. After several more days of riding, we saw signs of civilization.

Ahead of us we could see the outline of a double row of buildings and a goodly amount of stove smoke rising into the clear blue sky. The view to the west was marked by low hills offering a fair covering of grass greened up by the spring rains and, closer to the settlement, a valley with a glint of river water. Both the Yellowstone and the Tongue flowed through this area.

"I believe that must be Miles City, Mr. Gates, if the information those folks gave us a couple of days ago is correct. That means that you can be freed of your responsibility for my welfare. I have no real goal in mind so Miles City is as good a stopping place for me as anywhere.

"As long as they have a cafe or a mercantile where I can find honorable employment, I will be alright. I owe you a debt of gratitude, Mr. Gates. I know I've been a burden to you."

Mr. Gates took a quick glance my way and then looked toward the village. He said nothing for the longest time. Finally, "Whatever you wish. But you haven't been a burden. I've enjoyed your company." He then fell silent again.

I returned his silence with silence of my own. As we wound our way into the town I felt I had to say something more than thanks and good-bye. "Where will you be heading now, Mr. Gates? Are you still hoping to search for gold?"

He slumped back into his saddle and grinned over at

me, bracing himself with one hand on the horse's rump. He had mostly healed from the fight with Silas so the grin was almost natural. There was still a bit of deep blue coloring around his eye.

"It's a long ride to the Colorado high country but that's where the gold is. Or so they're saying around the saloons and gathering places. There's been mining in those hills for twenty years or more but I figure I'll be able to find just the right spot, a place that everyone else has missed; somewhere high up where I can dig gold and enjoy a downward view of the rest of the world at the same time, nothing above me but eagles.

"Since I have no one waiting for me or wondering about me I figure a summer in those hills might be just the thing to do. A slow ride south should have me in the high gold country in time to see the last of the melting snow. I expect I'll be able to scoop double handfuls of gold into a bucket and tote it down the mountain in canvas sacks and live rich and happy as Croesus forever more."

He then laughed out loud, the first time I had heard him laugh since I had enjoyed my little pity time a couple of weeks earlier. I liked the sound of it.

I found myself laughing with him. "I don't believe a word of that, Mr. Gates, and I doubt very much if you believe it either."

He feigned a serious look. "You've got to have some faith, Dora." But then he laughed again and we both knew he was on an adventure not a serious hunt for riches. If some gold found its way into a canvas sack, that would be a bonus.

I studied him again, a habit that had been growing stronger each day we were together. I had been wondering about something and finally got up the nerve to ask, "You say you have no one waiting for you or wondering about you. How does that come to be the case? Most folks have at least some family or a special someone."

Mr. Gates hunched his shoulders, a habit I had noticed several times.

"My folks are gone these past several years and my sister and two brothers are scattered across the country. Not too sure where any of them are.

"As for someone special, I've walked out with a girl from time to time but they soon grow tired of my clumsy ways. I'm not suited for the big city and I'm not house-broken enough for even most ranch cabins. I'm big and rough around the edges.

"I know my way around a camp, or a cattle drive, or a herd of horses but I never met a woman who wanted to subject herself to trying to tame me or teach me. I can't really blame them; there's easier targets. I've come to accept the situation."

I waited for him to finish speaking. Then, "I'm not one to argue or give advice, Mr. Gates, but I'm not sure you quite have the right of that. I know you have been a perfect gentleman on this trip even after I shot your coffeepot."

We both laughed and said no more. It was probably a good decision.

It was about noon on a dull and overcast day when we rode down the main street of the little settlement. The hand-painted sign at the end of the street announced, Miles City, population 950.

At first glance, it was difficult to see any real reason why those nine-hundred-fifty folks had chosen to stop here. There was just nothing at all attractive about the town itself although the hills to the west held a rugged beauty. Nevertheless, I was about to become the nine-hundred-fifty-first resident.

We slowly rode the three-block length of the main street and then turned around and rode back. Mr. Gates took in the entire town with the sweep of one arm. "See anywhere you might like to offer your services?"

"I'll try the newspaper first. I've set a bit of type and I might be able to sell some ads. If that doesn't work, I see a couple of mercantile stores and three or four restaurants.

"But first I need to find a boarding house that is fit and affordable. I'll never land a job looking like this, wearing men's pants, a checkered flannel shirt and a Stetson hat, all covered in dust, sagging from the rain and looking road weary. I'll get myself cleaned up and then make some calls."

We angled across the street and stopped in front of the sheriff's office. There were four men standing in a circle on the dirt road, one of them wearing a badge. They stopped talking and looked up as we approached.

I noticed one unshaven man in filthy range clothes looking me over. My skin crawled at his evil look.

Mr. Gates spoke to the sheriff, "Afternoon. We just arrived in town and the lady needs a decent boarding house. Can you direct us to such?"

The sheriff pushed his hat back and tipped his head towards the back streets of the little village. "Couple of boarding houses in town, good ones, too. Don't think any take couples though."

"We're not a couple. The lady has employed me to guide her across the prairie. I'll be moving on once she's settled."

The evil-looking man ran his eyes up and down me again and sneered. "Woman such as that, taking up with a man not her husband, might just as well go on over to Anna Turner's."

His comment left little doubt about what Anna Turner's was.

Mr. Gates dropped the reins of his horse and stepped to

the road. I knew what was coming and feared for him in a new town, not knowing how the sheriff might react.

"I'll handle this, Mr. Gates."

The men all looked at me. I had my little pistol out and aimed.

"Sheriff, if you will please just step back a bit, I'll have a clearer shot at this foul-mouthed, filthy man."

When the men saw me aiming the pistol at the sneering man, no one moved.

The sheriff clearly didn't know what to do. He just stood there looking bewildered.

Mr. Gates' voice sounded as stern as I had ever heard it, "I said the lady is a lady in every sense of the word. Anyone else has any foul talk, you'll answer to me."

He looked at the man who had done the talking. "For now, you owe the lady an apology and you had better make it sound like you mean it."

The man swallowed as if he had a lump in his throat. Lifting his hat clear of his head, he said, "Ma'am, I misspoke and I apologize. Don't know what got into me. It won't happen again."

The sheriff glanced my way but spoke to Mr. Gates, "Looks as if the lady can take care of herself."

Mr. Gates nodded at him. "Best you all remember that."

The sheriff pointed down a back street. "Ma'am, you need to talk to Bridgett O'Malley in that big white house over there."

I thanked the sheriff and Mr. Gates swung back into his saddle. It took but a few moments to ride to where we were directed. I was getting over my surprise at what had happened.

I glanced at Mr. Gates and giggled like a nervous school girl. "Mr. Gates, you are either a good teacher or I am a particularly ready student. I'm afraid I have slipped rather quickly into the ways of the frontier. I wasn't even shocked when you stepped out of the saddle and I knew what you were going to do. And then when I looked down I had my gun in my hand.

"I hope I wouldn't have shot that man but I'm not real sure any more."

"Have to do what needs doing, Dora."

At the boarding house I dismounted and passed my reins to Mr. Gates, then opened the picket gate and stepped up to the door. Just as I was about to knock to announce myself, the door opened and a slim, attractive lady stepped out, her red hair piled into a swirl atop her head. She barely glanced at me but focused her eyes on Mr. Gates. "Who's he? I don't allow any men in the house. If you're together, you can get right back on that horse and move along."

There was a bit of bite to her tone of voice and just a hint of a brogue that suggested a childhood in the old country.

I was so taken aback that I was stuck for words for a bit. I looked from the owner of that pile of red hair, out to Mr. Gates, and then back at the red hair.

"That is Mr. Gates. He has been my guide across the prairie for nearly three weeks and has shown himself to be a gentleman every minute of that time. I'll not hear you casting doubt on his honor, or mine either for that matter. But the fact is that once I am settled into suitable accommodations, Mr. Gates will be moving on and I doubt if you or I will ever see him again. That will be a loss for both of us as Mr. Gates has been good company and has shown integrity not often seen on this frontier.

"Now, if that's settled to your liking, tell me about the

accommodation you offer and the cost. And before you shake your red hair at me again, please understand that I am no shrinking violet. I prefer to be a gentlewoman and a lady but I can well speak up for myself when the need is clear."

A man's voice spoke up from behind me, someone I hadn't seen walking from around the house. "Ah, you're in trouble with this one, Bridgett O'Malley. You take her in, you'll be answering to her within the week. Better send her off to Mrs. Lacy, her that's afraid of her own shadow. She could benefit with some backbone around her house even if it isn't her own.

"Mind you, I've been waiting all these long months to see something like this; someone who could take the biting tongue and flashing eyes of Bridget O'Malley and give as well in return. It'll put a spring in my step even just seeing these past few moments." His grin was about to split his face open.

Mrs. O'Malley planted her fists on her rather flaring hips and gave the man a glare that would stop a grizzly in its tracks. "Your job is to see to the animals and the garden so go see to them. Be gone with you. I don't pay you to stand around or to offer your opinions on things that do not concern you."

The man remained standing where he was, that silly grin plastered across his face.

Mrs. O'Malley directed her stare at me and gave a casual wave at my riding attire. "Do you always dress in men's clothing? We would have to have an understanding on that. I take in and care for ladies. If you are a lady under all that dust and flannel, I have a room you could have for five dollars a week, meals included. You do your own laundry. If that horse needs boarding, it will cost you another dollar."

"Provided you are a good cook and your rooms are clean, Mrs. O'Malley, I find that to be satisfactory. But before we shake on it, I will have to see what I can do for employment. Is there a bathhouse in town where a lady can get cleaned up and be made presentable?"

"You can do that right here and you might just as well join me for lunch first, flannel or no flannel. I could give your Mr. Gates some lunch on the back stoop if he wished."

I looked out at Mr. Gates sitting like a king or emperor atop his horse and tried to imagine him squatting on the back stoop while Mrs. O'Malley fed him lunch. Chuckling to myself at that thought, I looked back at the landlady. "I'll just lead my horse around to your shed and unload him. I believe Mr. Gates is perfectly capable of caring for his own needs."

Mrs. O'Malley spoke to her hired man, "Walter, take the lady's horse around back and bring her bags in."

Turning to me as if she had to win at least one point in our rambling discussion, she asked, "I suppose you have a name. What would you like me to call you?"

A flippant answer floated to the front of my brain but I fought it down. "Dora. Just call me Dora and we will get along fine, on that point at least."

Just before stepping into the house, I turned to Mr. Gates. "Will you be staying for a bit, Mr. Gates, or is this good-bye?"

"I'll hang around for a couple of days. You can find me at the hotel or the livery if you need me. Good luck on the job search."

I had my lunch, my bath and my change of clothing, and headed to Main Street to inquire about employment. My first stop was the newspaper where I met Mr. Andrew Potter: a painfully-thin, balding, middle-aged man much stained by ink who described himself as the owner, reporter, typesetter, printer and salesman.

With a mischievous grin, he waved at the interior of his small shop. "I'm a slave to the news. There's no profit in it except the profit of an informed citizenry. So, what would make you hope that I could afford an employee? Even one who's visual presence would make the long dreary days a little less long and dreary? I am afraid, my dear, that you are digging for water in a dry hole. You might try Hobson's Mercantile. As sparing as that old miser is with his advertising budget, I expect he has sixty cents saved out of the first dollar he ever earned."

As if dismissing me, he turned back to the setting of type for his weekly addition. I pushed up my ruffled sleeves and picked up a composing stick. Turning a handwritten page so I could read it, I started to set it for printing. Mr. Potter glanced at me out of the corner of his eyes but said not a word. I completed one sentence only before laying the stick with its type on the table before him. I wiped the ink off my hands, picked up a printed order pad and pencil and stepped out of the shop. Neither of us had spoken.

Seeing a large sign announcing Hobson's Mercantile at the end of the street, I quickly walked that way. Within one-half hour, I was back in the newspaper office with a contract for a large ad to be run weekly for the next three months. I placed the contract before Mr. Potter and waited. It seemed a lengthy wait although it was probably only a minute or so.

"I wouldn't be able to pay you much."

"You will pay me fifty dollars a month, Mr. Potter, and be glad of it. I have to get settled at Mrs. O'Malley's boarding house this afternoon but I can start tomorrow. I will be here at eight o'clock."

He gave me a grim, trapped look. "I start at seven."

I returned my most radiant smile. "And I am sure that is a good decision, Mr. Potter. One that will no doubt lead you to fame and riches. I will see you at eight."

9

NOAH

AS I'VE SAID BEFORE, I'm a peaceful man. At least by preference. But you always have to make allowance for the situation.

After leaving Dora in Miles City, I pointed my horse's nose towards the gold hills. I had lost a bit of time guiding Dora across Dakota and Montana but after mulling it over, I finally admitted to myself that I had enjoyed her company. So the loss of time didn't really much matter. I would be a couple of weeks late in getting to the gold fields but I wasn't worried about it.

I appreciated Dora's cooking, too, and the fact that she had insisted on looking after the dishes and camp gear herself. That insistence had come after she rewashed some tin plates I had already hauled back from the creek. They looked fine to me but after picking up one that I had stowed away, she gave me an exasperated look.

"Mr. Gates, I hope you never decide to sign on as a

camp cook. I'm afraid your round-up crew would either all die of food poisoning or quit in despair."

I figured she had somewhat to learn about round-up crews but I let it go.

She continued though, "How would it be if you sit and visit with me while I care for the camp gear? You can return the favor by packing everything up for travel each day and saddling my horse."

That short speech was followed by a most charming smile.

You can't hardly argue with a woman like that so I chose a bit of grass and a likely looking small birch to lean against and watched her work.

Now, you can picture most riders sitting after dinner rolling a smoke but I had never taken up the habit. Having nothing to keep my hands busy, I cleaned and oiled my Colt and then pulled the Winchester carbine from the saddle scabbard and treated it to some kindness as well. Then I wiped the dust off all the shells in my belt as well as the ones in each gun.

I was remembering that and some other things as I left Miles City and made my way south and a bit further west.

Well, I finally reached Colorado and after some inquiry from folks around a little miners' supply town called Idaho Springs, I chose a hill to climb and a small creek to follow. There was no trail and only a few places where small amounts of rock had been broken which led me to believe that perhaps no one else had chosen this exact spot.

In my search for riches and solitude, I climbed higher than the last indication of work I had seen on the way up. I was at least eleven-thousand feet and maybe higher. The lack of breathable air made for a real tough climb there at the last. The horses and I were all having trouble getting breath into our lungs and Wolf lay down panting every chance he got, so rare was the atmosphere.

I had bought a gold pan in Idaho Springs although the store clerk had to show me how to use it. From comments he made, I got the feeling that he had done this before to other greenhorns. The look he gave me as I was leaving the store was probably pity but it might have been something else like the desire to take off his apron and come with me.

As I climbed along the little run of water, I stopped every once in a while to dip a pan, hoping to find even the smallest bit of color. In a bit of a back-eddy where the hillside leveled out for a few feet and the gravel sloped gently into the little stream, I found my first sign of gold. Not much. It would still leave me a far distance from riches. But gold is gold. I kept climbing and looking for three more days, finding tiny bits of color in nearly every pan.

The little run of water had narrowed down to just a few inches in width when it finally disappeared altogether into a mixture of low shrubbery, moss and ground vines at the base of a cliff. I pulled some ground moss and small bushes out of the way and found that the trickle was coming from a break under the nearly vertical granite wall.

I untied my shovel off the packhorse and started scraping the rock clean along where that trickle of water was running. In no time at all I had a patch ten-feet square cleared off. The granite was shattered and broken and laced with rust-stained white quartz. I then cleaned off a patch of the rock face and found the same situation; broken granite with rusty quartz filling each crooked void in the granite.

I unloaded the packhorse and tethered the two animals a short distance away. Digging into a pannier, I found my rock hammer. It took little effort to break away the fractured granite. The quartz was solid and strong.

When I had some granite broken off and cleared away, I used my pick to break off the protruding quartz. Right away I knew I had found gold. The chunk of quartz was laced with color. What quantity of mineral there was would not be known without doing a lot more digging.

I wasted no time and before long I had a pile of broken granite shoveled off to the side and several pieces of quartz laid carefully on a small ground sheet.

I knew I couldn't carry all that quartz down the mountain so I set aside several pieces that I found to be most attractive, like jewelry designed for the richest woman. The rest of the quartz I broke apart, scraping the gold into one of the small tanned leather bags I had bought from that same clerk in Idaho Springs.

Knowing the nature of man and the madness of his hunt for gold, I sat with my back to that granite wall and my weapons handy while I extracted the color from the quartz. I couldn't hide the sounds of my hammer striking rock. I could only hope the sound didn't attract an unwelcome visitor.

Of course, I had to admit to myself that I didn't really know what I was doing. Call it dumb luck or a blessing from God, or whatever you wish, but from the time I hit my first sign of color the digging just got better and better. It seemed no time at all until I had the first little sack filled with gold scratched out of the hillside. I chuckled when I thought about what I'd said to Dora about digging gold out by the bucket full. Well, I didn't actually use my bucket for digging as I needed it for water but you get what I mean.

Thinking further about Dora gave me a few minutes of regret while I considered that perhaps I should have done things differently. "Too late for that," I finally decided and got back to my digging.

I had to be careful to not overlook the small pieces of

color that got mixed up in the debris of the dig. I sifted and strained that rubble between my fingers, taking a good bit of skin off in the process. I hadn't thought to bring anything up the mountain with me that might do the job more efficiently.

The gold was in chunks embedded in virtually every piece of that gleaming white quartz. It was a sight to behold crumbling out of that fractured mountain rock. I had trouble holding down my excitement.

Some of those pieces would make fine jewelry just the way they were without any work from men's hands.

NOAH

I HAD SET up my camp just a few feet from that wall of quartz. The site offered a trickle of water, enough to keep me and the animals satisfied. Fed by the seeps and rivulets of the last of the melting snow, the grass had been greening and the wild flowers were making their frantic rush to blossom out before the short mountain summer again surrendered to the biting winds and falling snows of a Colorado high-country winter. It was a good camp.

Those high up hills held the promise of a peaceful if lonely summer in one of the most beautiful countries my mind could imagine. I was alright with the loneliness. I had lots of practice with being alone. All I wanted to do was spend the remaining days of the short summer digging out quartz and breaking the gold out of it. And enjoying the experience of the wilderness life. I offered no threat to anyone nor had I any intention of doing such as that.

After a couple of weeks of mixing stillness and hard

work, I even half forgot about the loss of my G-bar horses. Somewhere in my jumbled thoughts about those lost horses there was still a lot of anger. I had no idea what to do about the anger and had no real hope of ever seeing my horses again.

With the horses mostly out of my mind and with the peace and beauty all around me, I found myself thinking more and more about Dora and wondered how she was doing way up there in Miles City.

Until I spent that winter in Deadwood I knew nothing at all about searching for gold. But you spend enough time pouring coffee for the old-timers and listening to their tales, a man picks up some things.

"There's other signs fer gold, young feller, but the simplest fer a pilgrim is to look fer veins of quartz in the bedrock."

A bewhiskered, skinny rail of a man laid that wisdom on me one bitter cold night after drinking so much coffee I got to wondering where he stored it all.

"Now, ya got t' understand that don't work every time. Could be you'll use up a week or two of yer life mov'n rock and have noth'n t' show fer it but a hole in the ground. From time to time though, if'n yer liv'n a good clean life and ya bin remember'n to pray fer yer Mama, the clouds will part fer ya and you'll come up with some color.

"That should happen, don't you be shout'n and holler'n like some of these fools do. You do that, you'll bring diggers to yer claim like flies t' a picnic. My advice, just keep yer mouth shut and keep digg'n."

It was following his instructions and the panning advice of that store clerk that had directed me to the spot I was in.

Well, when I saw that jewelry rock exposed out of the crumbling granite, you better believe I felt like shouting but I remembered what the old-timers had said and kept quiet as I rolled that piece of quartz over and over in my hands, marveling at the beauty and the promise of it.

It wasn't easy digging but that whole cliff face as well as the rock floor I was standing on was a treasure-house of color. I ignored everything but the quartz, chipping away the granite until the white rock could be broken out. I had no way of knowing how deep the quartz went into the granite and no way to break it out so I just worked on the surface.

I was alone all summer up there in that rocky confine with only the canopy of a beautiful blue sky above me and almost daily thunder and rainstorms that sent me scurrying for my tent. A high-country thunderstorm is a memorable event. In spite of the storms and the difficult digging, I was setting aside a good amount of pay rock and had several filled-up leather sacks tucked into my panniers.

On clear nights, I didn't bother with the tent, simply rolling my bed out under the shelter of the starry sky. I had done so on this night I'm getting set to tell you about.

I was having a peaceful sleep, unaware of the false dawn that was breaking over the eastern horizon, when something prodded my shoulder.

I came near to jumping out of my skin at that unexpected touch. My eyes opened and the first thing I saw was the muzzle of a carbine a few inches away, gaining my attention and forcing me into a decision. I had started to sit up but one look at that rifle bore and the grinning, vacant-eyed face of the man holding it and I lay back down just as quiet as you please.

As I lay back, I wondered where Wolf was and how the intruder had gotten this close without me hearing a warning. The dog had taken to wandering a bit after I pitched my camp, sometimes disappearing for several hours. He must have been off on business of his own on this early morning but, about that time, he arrived back in camp. His warning growl caused the intruder to swing his weapon towards the animal but he was too late to stop Wolf from sinking sharp teeth into his arm.

The gunman let out with a bloodcurdling scream that must have echoed all around the mountaintop. I didn't pay it much mind though; I was too busy trying to get out of my bedding and away from the tumbling mass of man and animal.

Truth to tell, I couldn't rightly say just exactly what happened next. I do know that among the terrified screams of Wolf's victim and the threatening shouts of a second gunman, I was soon out of my blankets fumbling my Colt out of my tangled-up bedding when a searing pain ripped through the muscle of my left arm just above my elbow. The pain was followed by the sound of a shot and almost immediately by another shot. Where that second bullet went I have no idea but it didn't hit me for which I am most certainly grateful.

By this time, I had the Colt in hand and was getting squared around. Wolf now had a grim grip on the leg of the one gunman so I turned and snapped off a lucky shot at the second man.

That shot took him in the shoulder but by that time my second bullet was on its way. I watched as the gunman's face disappeared in a mess of blood and gore. He crumpled to the ground at the edge of my camp clearing and I turned to the man that Wolf had in his grip.

I was just in time to see the gunman free his carbine and swing a brutal club stroke that connected with Wolf's head. Wolf let go of his leg grip and collapsed into the grass. The gunman was raising the carbine in my direction when my shot took him three inches above his belt buckle. I was still lying on my back so the shot traveled upwards into his vitals doing damage all along the way.

All the fight left him. It just seemed to seep out and leave him as limp as an empty burlap bag. He slowly sat down on the grass, gripped his stomach and rolled over on his side, blood flowing freely from between his fingers.

The gunman was a long-haired, bearded, dirty threat of a man showing no promise towards civility. Scared, he was, laying there in the grass knowing he was dying. His face was a mask of pain. He pulled his knees up tight to his stomach and then stretched out straight, then pulled them back up as if he was looking for some kind of release from the terrible damage the .45 slug had done.

Trembling, I finally got to my feet and stepped over to the first man I had shot. He was clearly dead so I made my way back to the second man. I knelt beside him. "Can you hear me? There's nothing I or anyone else can do for you but you might give me your name and I'll pass word on to any kin who might wonder about you."

I waited for a part of a minute with no response. Finally, he mumbled through lips that were now covered in bubbly, foaming blood. "Turk Sommers. That other is my brother, Bev. Ma ain't gonna be happy. Not happy at all. We promised to come back with gold. But we just had no luck."

"So you decided to steal mine, is that it?"

I don't think he heard me.

Again, he whispered, "Ma ain't gonna be happy." He died there, just like that.

So there I stood in my long johns and stocking feet with a bleeding arm that was starting to really hurt, a dog that lay unconscious, and two dead men.

I hadn't even had my morning coffee yet or put on my

pants. And now my long johns had a ragged bullet hole in the arm, too; they weren't going to see me through the rest of the season at this rate.

Fall was still a couple of weeks away but there was a serious nip in the air the past few mornings and there was no denying that the short summer would soon become a blustery fall. It frightened me to think what would become of anyone foolish enough to allow themselves to become trapped up here if their frantic, greedy digging for gold tricked them into ignoring the warning of what was to come. Maybe it was time to pack up and ride down the mountain. I would need doctoring on my arm anyway and I had a pretty good stash of gold bagged up.

I used my one good arm to drag the two dead men away from camp and went for the pick and shovel. It was brutally hard going in that rocky ground with just the one good arm but I finally scratched out a hole big enough to hold the two gunmen. I rolled them into the grave one at a time after going through their pockets and piling their gather on my blanket. I shoveled rock and dirt over the bodies making good use of the pile of shattered granite, tamped it all down with the back of the shovel and the heel of my boot, and stood back. I wiped the sweat off my brow and said, "That's as much as either of you deserve."

I was in no mood for sermonizing, giving or receiving, either one. Anyway, I'd have to admit to being a little short of knowledge on those things and doubted that those two boys knew any more about it than I did. So I whacked the grave again with the back of the shovel and figured that was a good enough eulogy given the circumstances.

By that time, my arm was thundering with pain and Wolf was awake, staggering around camp like a drunk. I still hadn't had my coffee and burying dead men is thirsty work. So I went to the little stream that had kept me and my animals in water all summer and washed the blood and grime off my hands, then built up the fire and put coffee water on. I considered pulling my sore arm out of the cotton long john sleeve but finally lifted my knife from its sheath and cut the bloody piece of cloth off, dropping it into the fire.

The arm was a mess and the digging of the grave hadn't done it one bit of good. It was puffy and swollen and red-rimmed an inch around the bullet hole. But the good news was that the lead had gone right through without hitting the bone and the bleeding had slowed to a trickle. That was the only good thing about the entire morning I could think of; that and the fact that I wasn't dead.

I heated water in a pot and washed the arm as well as I could, then wrapped it in the cleanest cloth I could find. I built up my fire again, put on my cleanest dirty shirt, and figured I was about ready for the day.

I set about gathering some breakfast together and put the shooting of the Sommers boys out of my mind, figuring they hadn't left me much choice.

It occurred to me that Dora would have had something to say about how I treated my wound. That woman did feel free to express an opinion from time to time although I had never let it bother me.

Within an hour, I was packed up and ready to head down the trail. I knew I hadn't dug out the entire deposit and was leaving gold behind but these hills had gold hidden in many places. If someone found my camp and grew wealthy from further digging, well, 'good on 'em'. I didn't figure to ever be coming back. I left the shovel and pick and a few other tools right where they were, leaning on the rock face beside my little gold mine. If someone were to come across them and put them to use, they'd be welcome. Anyway, the shovel handle was broken and only poorly tied back together, and both the pick and my rock hammer were dulled down where there were no points left.

I had been camped high up on a little water run that was a tributary to Clear Creek. I hadn't seen a living soul all summer long but I heard hammers striking steel from time to time and, on a rare occasion, the echo of blasting powder. The miners working the steel drills were far enough away that we didn't bother each other.

I had done my digging with pick and shovel. The mountain of rock above me all appeared to be the same seamed and crumbling granite I had been working on. I figured that rock face could be brought down with just a small bit of powder but I put it out of my mind, figuring I might display my ignorance of the stuff by blasting the entire hillside down on my head. I couldn't see much benefit coming from such as that.

It's doubtful if anyone heard the slight noise of my work but they would have heard the echo of an occasional shot from my carbine as I pulled in a deer or two and once, an elk. I was surprised the elk was up that high but there he was like a gift just as I was coming to need meat. I skinned him out and stretched the green hide over my diggings to add a bit of shade and a partial shelter from the frequent rains after wrapping the meat in some well-waxed cloth I had for the purpose.

It took me the most of the day to get off that hillside, picking my way down the mountain where no real trail existed. But by early evening I was in Idaho Springs, a sprawling collection of wood frame buildings that were gradually giving way to more permanent brick and stone.

The trail I was following led me right onto a flat spread of land laid out between the surrounding mountains. The town existed for the sole purpose of supplying the miners.

There were indications of mining everywhere I looked. Mines as small as hand-dug, rocky, heartbreak holes to big operations that dominated whole hillsides with their buildings rising up in stages like stair steps, conforming to the slope of the land.

My bullet-shot arm had settled down to a dull throb as the day went along but it would still need doctoring. I figured that could wait until I had talked with the sheriff and got myself some supper. I put my saddle horse and my two packhorses up in the livery barn, paid the hostler extra to help Wolf keep an eye on them, and walked the two Sommers boys' horses over to the marshal's office.

Without hardly even thinking about it, I checked horse brands everywhere I went hoping to see a G-bar that would mark it as my animal. I guess I hadn't put those horses as far out of my mind as I thought I had.

The deputy was sweeping the walk outside the small law office and jail. I tied the Sommers boy's horses to the hitch rail and asked about the sheriff. The deputy leaned on his broom and nodded across the dirt road. "He takes his supper about this time every day. I'd suggest you wait here for him though. He purely hates to have his supper interrupted."

I nodded my understanding and walked across the road. I hadn't talked with another human person for months and the thought of it set me up a bit so I stepped right along. Anyway, sheriff or no sheriff, I was hungry myself.

There was only one man in the cafe wearing a badge so my unspoken question answered itself.

I lay my carbine across an unused table, pulled up a chair and ordered a coffee and a meal. I leaned towards the man with the badge. "Evening, Sheriff. I've a little piece of work for you when you're done with that steak."

He placed his fork on his plate and looked at me. I folded my elbows on the table and thumbed back my hat, giving him a tired grin.

"Just a small piece of work, Sheriff, and there's no big hurry to it. The men are already dead and buried so I don't expect anything is going to change in the time it takes for the both of us to eat our suppers."

I saw several heads come up and folks staring my way.

The sheriff picked up his fork and spoke around a mouthful of grease-fried beef. "This hour of my day don't belong to the town or the county, either one. I don't do business during supper hour. You come to the office later and we'll talk."

I continued grinning at him. "I'll think on that, Sheriff. I may take a notion to ride on before an hour is up and then you'll never know whose horses those are tied up in front of your shop. Of course, what I decide to do will all depend a bit on how long it takes me to eat and then find a doctor who can plug up this bullet hole in my arm.

"Won't be riding on until all of that is done. Then I might go for a drink. So thinking on all that I guess there's time enough alright. You could probably track me down in the saloon were you of a mind to."

The sheriff went back to his meal for a moment or two but finally curiosity got the better of him. "Who shot you and why?"

"We'll talk later, Sheriff. I hate to disturb a man at his food." I was grinning inside but managed to sound serious.

"You already disturbed me so you might just as well come out with the rest of it."

The girl came with my meal before I got a chance to tell my story so I commenced eating.

The sheriff looked my way and simply said, "Well?"

This time I grinned openly. "I hate to be disturbed

while I'm eating, Sheriff. We'll talk later." I heard a man chuckle from across the room.

Frustrated, the sheriff put his fork and knife down again and leaned towards me. "I expect you're having a bit of fun at my expense, fella, but that's alright. I've learned that after a summer alone in the hills you boys are apt to arrive in town just a little off center in your minds. But when you talk of a bullet hole in your arm and two dead men in the hills, you get my attention. So talk to me."

I swallowed, put my fork down and talked, using as few words as possible. I told the story so's everyone in the cafe could hear. The sheriff listened silently until I finished and then asked, "Got any names?"

"One of them said they were brothers. Turk Sommers and his brother, Bev. Said something about their Ma wasn't going to be happy with all of this. Well, I can understand her not being happy about losing two sons as good for nothing as they were. But whether she's around here and a part of their thievery I have no way of knowing. Perhaps you know the family, Sheriff."

"I know them," said a man from two tables away. "Those boys live with an old woman they call Ma down the crick about ten mile or so. Hog dirty and lazy. Always looking for something that's not tied down that they might latch on to. Sounds like they latched onto too much this time. The world's a better place for it."

The sheriff nodded at this information. "I suppose I'm going to have to ride out there in the morning, see this Ma, and break the bad news. But what about you?" he asked, looking at me. "Why should I believe your story? I don't know you nor the Sommers boys, either one."

I took another bite of my steak. "Well, Sheriff, I'm the one sitting here talking to you. I'm the one with the bullet hole and I'm the one that brought those two horses down from the hills. I could have just kept riding and not said anything at all. Seems evidence enough to me but if you want, I'll draw you a map and you can go dig up those boys. You'll find all the bullet holes are in the front."

The sheriff put his fork down, pushed his chair back and reached for the makings. "Naw, it's out of my town jurisdiction anyway. I guess we'll just let er lay."

So we left it like that and the next morning after a bath and some new clothes and a night in a hotel bed, I was riding towards Denver. The doctor had cleaned up my bullet-damaged arm and advised me to keep it in a sling for a while. That didn't work out well, what with me having to hold the lead for the packhorses, so by the middle of the first day I gave up on the sling. I paid for that decision with some pain but a man has to do what has to be done.

NARRATOR

THE BARGER GANG was riding twelve strong towards a little cattle town in Kansas. The town was small but the bank was stuffed full of cash. Or so the story had been told to Barger.

A week earlier, Barger had been sitting at a table in a saloon in Dodge with Obie Trembley, a full-time gambler and sometimes informant. Barger leaned forward and whispered, "You sent for me. What've you got?"

Trembley matched Barger's posture and softly said, "Way I hear it, the bank down to Wayside is stuffed to the rafters with a cattle buyer's cash and just begging to be took. Have to be quick though. The buyer is already there and the cattle are on the move. You got the boys stashed anywhere close to down there?"

Barger ignored the question, taking a long study of the gambler. Finally, "This good information?"

"Good as gold."

"Would you stake your life on it?"

There was a silent pause and then, "Barger, every time I talk to you I'm putting my life on the line. Don't know why I do it."

"You do it for the money I pay you and not anything else. Now, would you stake your life on this information you've just given me? You're asking me and the boys to stake our lives so now I'd need to know how tight your story is before we ride in there."

Trembley leaned back in his chair, looked across the table at Barger and picked up his shot glass, twirling it in his fingers for just a moment. "It's good enough that I wish I could ride with you."

Barger pushed his chair back. "I'll be coming to see you one way or the other. Either I'll have some folding bills for you or a bullet. Best you hope we're successful." He got up and walked out into the sunshine.

Three days later, the cattle buyer was taking his ease, his cash was in the bank, the herds were on the trail and Barger and his boys were a short five miles away.

Barger was always cautious but there was no way to prevent the dust storm kicked up by a dozen horses.

A cowboy just a mile to the west was curious about the dust cloud. Any excuse to escape the boredom of herding cattle was an opportunity too good to pass up. He rode to a small hilltop to take a look. He decided right away that twelve well-armed men riding in a tight bunch spelled trouble. Everyone in town was aware of the situation with the buyer and the cash in the bank, including the curious cowboy.

The cowboy, looking at the hard-charging men below him, was immediately suspicious. Hidden by the rolling hills, he spurred his horse into a run towards town, pulling up breathlessly in front of the sheriff's office and hollering out even before his horse had come to a stop. "Dan, Dan, get your butt out here."

The sheriff stepped out of the office. "What's all the noise about Kelly? You're acting like you seen a ghost."

"Not a ghost, a gang. That is if my eyes are still working proper. Twelve well-armed hard-cases heading this way in a bunch, maybe a couple of miles south of town. Looks like trouble to me. I got to thinking about that cattle money we've all been hearing about. Could be the news got out and these boys are coming for it."

Dan swung into action immediately. "You spread the word to the north end of town. I'll go this way. Get every man you can and meet at the livery. And hurry."

Dan hollered for his deputy, "Barney, get your lazy self out here." Barney didn't hear though; he wasn't there. Not waiting for an answer, the sheriff went off to holler up the townsmen.

Within ten minutes there were thirty excited men spread out in the livery barn, hunkered down below the creek bank, and under the single bridge that led into town from the south road. The cattle buyer was among them with a holstered .45 Colt and a Winchester carbine carried with authority as if he had done this before. The men were carrying everything from old cap and ball pistols to .22 cal. rabbit guns to Sharps buffalo guns to modern Winchester carbines. "Hide yourselves well, men," the sheriff hollered. "Protect yourselves. We don't want any of us hurt. And no shooting until we know who they are. I'll make that decision and take the first shot if it becomes necessary. Quiet now!"

But there was just no way thirty excited and scared men were going to remain quiet. As it happened it didn't really matter. All the hard-riding gang could hear was the pound of their own horse's hooves plus the wind in their ears and the thumping of their own hearts.

As the gang rode around the last curve in the trail with the town sheltered from view by the livery haystacks, Sheriff Dan Ledger stepped into the center of the road just as it led off the two-track bridge. "Hold up there, men." His shouting voice was lost in the pound of hooves but the gang saw him well enough, standing tall with his arms raised to the sides. The Winchester in his right hand was clearly visible as well. There could be no doubt as to the meaning of his being there.

The next few seconds were a blur of swirling dust, shouting men, and screaming horses as riders pulled cruelly on reins.

Barger, not normally one to take unnecessary risks, pulled his horse to a stop and signaled for his men to do likewise. But one hot-headed rider shouted out, "We ain't stopping for just the one man. Shoot him down and let's ride."

Barger turned in his saddle to quiet the shouting man but it was too late. Willard Styles, the saddle maker and harness man, stepped into view, his Winchester rising for a shot. A gang rider threw a pistol shot at him, hitting his leg and dropping him to the ground. Suddenly there were men stepping into view from what seemed like every direction. Sheriff Dan, the decision to shoot taken out of his hands, dove head first off the bridge, landing in the mud at the side of the tiny creek. The shooting was instant and nonstop, bullets flying in every direction. Badly outnumbered and outshot, the gang broke and fled leaving three men lying on the dusty trail. In less than a minute, it was all over.

The milling riders pulled themselves together and fled back the way they had come. It was every man for himself until Barger managed to spur his horse to the front of the pack and take over the leadership again. There was no pursuit. The townsmen had been given barely enough time to find a weapon and run to the livery and no time at all to gather horses.

The men slowly emerged from their hiding places and gathered around the mud-covered sheriff who was standing over the corpse of one of the riders. Three gang members lay on the road, two clearly dead and one with his arms wrapped around his middle as if he was trying to hold his innards together. The man was softly whimpering and clearly dying.

One man had run for the doctor while two men carefully lifted the wounded saddle maker into the back of a small wagon they had manhandled into place. No other townsmen had been injured.

Slim, the bartender from the saloon, pointed towards town, grinning from ear to ear. "Well, looky there at what's coming."

Everyone turned to where Slim was pointing to see Deputy Barney running towards them wrestling with his galluses with one hand and trying to tuck in his shirttail with the other, his Winchester flopping awkwardly under his arm.

"Where y'all been?" Slim asked unnecessarily. "Nothing left here to do," he said with an infectious grin. "Might just as well go back to the little house and finish up with that Montgomery Ward catalogue I seen you carrying out there." The men hooted and laughed but Barney didn't look as if he was enjoying the joke.

The Barger gang kept up a run for three miles before pulling behind a hill and stepping down from the saddle. "Get down, men. Give our horses a break. Water just over there." He left it to the men to figure out where 'there' was.

While the men went to relieve their thirst, Mason Benson who acted as the sometimes second in command to Barger, walked over, leading his exhausted mount. "Three men down and left behind, boss. The boys ain't likely to be happy about that."

"There's risks. Always is. I don't know how it came that they were waiting for us but that's how it is sometimes. Every man knows the risks of this game. If any want to pull out and get a job riding night herd on someone else's cattle or clerking in a store, ain't no one going to stop them.

"Now water your animal and let him graze for a bit. We've got miles to go. And, Mason, if you want to act as second here taking a leadership position, you better start acting like a leader. I got no place for a whiner. Now get someone watching up on that hill yonder. We don't want anyone surprising us with a visit."

Mason simply nodded and led his horse to the stream.

After a half-hour rest, Barger spoke out, "Gather around here men." When the riders were within earshot, he spoke, "You men know that I hate to lose a rider and I surely hate to leave one behind. But we couldn't have gathered those boys up without losing more of us. I think they were all dead so we couldn't have done anything for them anyway. That don't mean I like it. It's just the way of it. Now mount up and keep a sharp eye out for dust on our back trail."

There was no need for the gang to worry about a visit from a posse. Back in the little sun-drenched cow town, the sheriff stood with the other men watching the last of the gang hightail it down the trail back the way they had come. "Thanks, men. You got here just in time and stood your ground exactly right. The excitement is over so you can get back to whatever you were doing."

A voice from the gathered group asked loudly, "Ain't we going after them? Seems to me we could still catch them."

The sheriff spotted the speaker. "Walt, it makes no sense to chase them. They broke no laws and done the town no harm. They lost three of their own. Enough is enough."

Walt was still not satisfied. "Done the town no harm? What about Willard, him that's lying bleeding in the back of that wagon? He may have a different feeling about that."

Dan looked over at the wounded man and smiled. "Why, Walt, you and everyone else in town will be providing Willard free drinks for the next year, him telling about his heroism here today and pulling up his pant leg to show off his scar. Before long, the story will be that he stood off a vicious gang of thieves and half the Comanche Nation all at the same time and all by himself. That little scratch is the best thing ever happened to Willard."

The men laughed while Willard gave the sheriff a withering look and asked, "Where's that doctor?"

NARRATOR

WITH A BLUE-COATED, grim-faced guard walking on each side, Hank Ransom shuffled down the grungy corridor that led to Warden Gregg's office. The last time Hank had been through that door was three years before, the day he arrived at the New Mexico Territorial Prison. That time he had been shackled, had been wearing the filthy range clothes he was arrested in, and was scared half to death although he put on the bravest face he could muster. His arrest, trial and imprisonment had happened so fast he was still having trouble sorting it all out.

One minute he had been selling a horse to the man standing at the bar beside him and the next minute a complete stranger lay dead at his feet. The stranger had staggered and bumped into him from behind, spilling his beer down Ransom's shirt sleeve and down his own pant leg. When Ransom turned around to see who had bumped him, the man made a half-drunken remark about the horse trader smelling like the livery stable. Ransom tried to ignore him but the stranger suggested rather strenuously that the saloon would benefit from having one less stinking horse trader in it and challenged Ransom to a fight. Neither man was armed. Ransom was a thick, broad-shouldered, hard-muscled man well known for his strength.

The drunk ignored all of that and took a foolish-looking boxer's stance just before he swung an erratic right hand that missed Ransom by inches. Ransom reluctantly responded with a right of his own more in self-defense than in anger. His fist connected like the kick of a mule. The challenger's mouth and nose exploded in a chaos of blood and gore. It was all over. The man stood for a slow second - his brain punctured with shards of shattered bone - before he faded and crumbled to the floor.

Everyone in the saloon hollered self-defense but the dead man turned out to be the brother-in-law to the small-town sheriff and the local judge was a close friend. Hank Ransom found himself standing before an improvised court the next morning. The judge pounded his badly-scarred desk with the carpenter's hammer he used for a gavel. "Three years and count yourself lucky. And one word out of you and it becomes five."

Now, three years later on this visit to the warden's office, he was dressed in a cheap prison-issue, off-the-shelf suit with a white shirt and a narrow blue tie. A guard gave two light taps to the pebbled glass with 'Warden' written in white paint, waited a few seconds and then twisted the door knob. The warden lifted his eyes from the stack of papers on his desk. "Sit down, Ransom."

Hank Ransom remained standing holding his small canvas duffle bag in his left hand and said nothing.

The warden exhaled an exasperated breath and shook his head. "Stubborn right to the end are you, Ransom? Well, I can't say as I'm surprised. I don't believe you've said a hundred words in your three years here. You're the least talkative man I've ever known and maybe the strongest. Not that I mind your silence. At least you never gave me any lip although I often wondered what was going around in your head. But it's that bull strength that put you in here and will bring you back if you don't control it. You've controlled it for your time here and I hope that can continue.

"You can stand if you wish. Makes no never mind to me."

The warden stood up, reached past the stack of paper and picked up a single sheet that was laying by itself on the far edge of the desk. "Your time is up, Ransom. You're a free man at noon today. That's twenty minutes from now. Just as soon as you sign this paper, the guard will escort you to the gate and we'll all hope to never meet again. Not here anyway."

The warden lay the paper down on the only clear patch on the desk top. "Sign here."

Ransom reached for the pen the warden held out to him and slowly wrote his name on the bottom line. He passed the pen to the warden and stepped back a single pace. The warden picked up another piece of paper, this one with the name of the prison printed in a bold scroll across the top and under that in smaller type, 'The State of New Mexico'. "This is your discharge, Ransom. Put it in a safe place. You may need to prove your right to freedom if some glory-hound sheriff drags you into his office."

The warden held out the discharge paper and said, "Ransom, I never pretend to be friends with any of the men under my care but I hope to not be an enemy either. We're all just doing what has to be done. Will you shake?"

Ransom gave the man a slow study as he folded the discharge paper and slid it into the inside pocket of his jacket. Finally, he reached out and gave the offered hand a quick shake. The warden's hand was lost inside Ransom's huge fist. There were no further words, no smiles and no offers of 'luck to you'.

Warden Gregg picked up two gold pieces off the desk and held them out. "This is your discharge money. It's not much but it's enough for a train ticket if you're not going too far or a cheap horse if that's your traveling preference."

A guard indicated that the meeting was over and Ransom turned to the door. A word from the warden stopped him, "One more thing, Ransom. The world has changed in three years. You'll see some differences. Take your time to get used to them. Every sheriff has a telephone now and no horse was ever bred that could outrun that infernal contraption. There's some other changes, too. Well, you'll see it all soon enough."

With that, the warden sat down and again turned to the pile of paper on the desk. Ransom and the guards walked to the gate which swung open as they approached. The guards stopped and Hank Ransom kept walking, never once looking back. Still no words had been spoken. The guards watched until the released prisoner turned a corner on the dusty street and disappeared from sight.

Hank Ransom walked the short two miles from the prison into Santa Fe letting the idea of fresh air, open skies and freedom soak into him. The scorching, late summer sun beat down on his shoulders and bare head. He ignored the discomfort as well as the sweat that was building up under his shirt and threatening to soak into the prison-issue suit jacket. The thought of freedom and home overrode the heat and the blister that was forming on his heel.

Home. Sarah. Ezekiel, his son whom he called 'Zeke'. And the new child who was born after he was sent to prison and whom he had never seen. Sarah had written, telling about the baby she had named Toby. He was nearly three years old and had never known a father.

Was it all still there? Were they all still there? Had she really waited? The few letters he had received, dictated by Sarah but written by Rev. Wallaby, had assured him that she was waiting. The last letter written in a childish print was by Sarah's own hand. The reverend had apparently been teaching her to read and write. The short note read: "The three years seem like fifty but it is nearly over. Zeke is seven years old now and Toby will be three in a few months. Please hurry home."

In Santa Fe, Ransom stepped into the shaded coolness of a small trading post. The Mexican trader watched him approach with a wary, knowing eye. Hank set his small duffle on the countertop and said, "Need an outfit. Range clothes. Pants, shirt, long handles. Have to be cheap. Don't have much money. You want to see my release form?"

The trader shrugged his shoulders and his flowing mustache expanded the smile growing in his hidden lips. "No, Senor. I know the suit and tie. Only released men wear such foolish things. New Mexico, she don't do you any favor with these clothes. You wish to change them, yes?"

Hank slipped out of the suit jacket, laid it across the counter and said, "Just as soon as possible. But I don't like to put on new clothes without I first have a bath. You got a rain barrel or something I can use?"

"Ah, is good," the trader said. Beckoning with his arm, he led Hank towards the loading dock out back. On the dock, he pointed Hank to a barrel standing in the shade of the overhang. "There is soap and towel. You wash quick, not too many people see. I will bring you new clothes. What color you like?"

Hank nodded his thanks. "Don't much care about color. Care about the cost though."

The barrel was about half-full so Hank had to bend far in to scoop up each dipperful of water. Still, it took just a few minutes for the prison stink to be washed off and he was soon standing in his new canvas pants and checked wool shirt. He had done a hurry-up job of drying, rushed on by a team and wagon carrying a family, the kids laughing and pointing. Hank pretended he didn't see them as they made their way down the alley behind the stores.

He kept the prison shoes. He carried the ugly prison suit to the front counter of the trading post, dumping it on the floor. "You make anything of that, you're welcome." He paid for his purchases and dropped the change into a pocket.

Hank started to walk. His sense of freedom along with the washing away of the prison stink and the new range clothes seemed to put a bit of a bounce in his step. He walked only the short distance from the trading post to the Atlantic and Pacific Railway depot. At the depot, he asked the fare to Gallup. He paid over the money and tucked his ticket into his shirt pocket. The train wouldn't leave for several hours. The purchase of the ticket left him nearly broke.

Walking out on the station platform, he found a Mestizo woman grilling small chunks of beef wrapped in hand-formed fry bread and offering the food for sale. He counted the small coins she asked for and was given two pieces passed to him on a tin plate. There was nothing left of his release money so he contented himself with a drink from the station well. Coffee would have to wait until he arrived home.

After a long night sitting and sleeping on the hard wooden bench in the passenger car, Hank arrived in Gallup at noon the next day. There was no one to meet him at the station but he hadn't been expecting anyone. The walk to his small shack where his wife and children lived took him a half-hour. There he was met by a joyfully screaming woman who flew out of the house and into his arms, taking a steel grip around his chest and slathering him with kisses. Looking over her shoulder he saw his two children shyly watching from inside the humble home. The boys wouldn't know him. It would take some time to put the family back together again.

The reunited couple spent the next two days discussing the future. Money wasn't an immediate problem. Their herd of horses had been sold after Hank had gone to prison, adding the proceeds of the sale to their small savings. Hank kept another account in a Denver bank which remained untouched.

Sarah poured them each another cup of coffee and took her seat beside Hank on the small porch. "Your folks wrote that they would like you to come home. I can get the letter if you like."

"I don't need the letter. Just tell me what all they had to say. We never got along very well and I doubt as how Pa will ever get over having his son in prison."

Sarah put her cup down on the little table and leaned towards her husband. "They never mentioned prison in the letter. Just said they were starting to feel their age and the ranch could use a strong hand."

Hank sat silently sipping his coffee for several minutes. Finally, he reached for Sarah's hand. "Let's at least go and spend some time up there. The kids should meet their grandparents and you should get to know them better, too. Maybe there's something there for us. We'll have to see."

Within a matter of hours, they had packed up their few belongings and had the wagon wheels greased. The next morning, they were heading for Canyon View, Colorado.

13

NOAH

A RIDER on a fast horse could cover the distance from Idaho Springs to Denver in a single day if he was intent on getting there in a hurry. I wasn't in a hurry and Sam, my riding animal, was only average fast. I was also leading two heavily-laden packhorses. I figured three days for the trip. For mutual protection, I had hoped to find a group of miners heading out for the winter months but it seemed most of them were intent on pushing the season to its last snow-free day. So I had set out alone, careful every step of the way. I carried my Winchester across the saddle bows the whole time.

My first night out, I camped in a hollow in the hills away from prying eyes, hoping to have no one challenge me for my gold like the Sommers boys had done. On the second evening, I was looking for an opportunity to get off the trail when I spotted an opening between two group-ings of aspen with a little creek running between them. I walked my horses over the gravel bank of the creek, leaving only ill-defined tracks. Thinking I would be alone and sheltered for the night, I continued for half a mile. Just as Sam raised his head and lifted his ears, I smelled wood smoke. I pulled up, considering my options. Tempted to turn back and look for another camp, I was just in the process of turning Sam when I heard the cocking of a carbine hammer. When you've heard that sound once, you never forget. That click carried with it a whole group of messages starting with 'don't make any foolish moves'.

I carefully placed my hands one on top of the other on the saddle horn, my own weapon pointed away from the challenger, and settled back in the seat. "You're calling the deal, friend. Speak out."

A half-dozen careful steps carried the gunman into my line of sight. He was not overly tall but his shoulders were wide and his chest was thick. He looked to be strong as an ox. I'm a big man myself but I felt small studying this man.

"No need for the weapon, friend. I'm just searching out a camping spot for the night. Big country. I'll gladly move on."

"What is it Hank?" A pretty but tired-looking woman stepped up beside the gunman, a child holding each of her hands.

"Go back to the camp, Sarah." The woman stood where she was.

Seeing the woman and kids I figured this for a traveling family. It was unlikely they meant any harm. I took one hand slowly off the saddle horn and lifted my hat. "Sorry, ma'am. I didn't go to startle y'all. I'm just looking for a place to bed down for the night. Far as that goes, I pose no threat. I've a fresh shot buck on that packhorse. It's small but I figure we could share and I'd still have enough to see me to Denver."

The man stood silently studying me. I could see the doubt in his eyes that I figured was fear for his family.

The woman finally made the decision. "Hank, a little venison would go awful well with the bit we have in the pot."

After another minute's study, the man said, "Step down careful if you've a mind to. You wish to move on, that's fine too."

I stepped to the ground and walked towards the small family, leading the three horses. "Noah Gates, folks, making my way towards the big city. I'll share your fire if you're comfortable with that. If you'd rather I move on, that's alright too. We'll divide that venison and I'll be on my way."

The man tucked the carbine into the crook of his arm. "Hank Ransom. My wife Sarah. You care for your animals. I'll lift that meat down to where Sarah can get what she needs." He didn't introduce the boys.

The boys were all set to make friends with Wolf. I spoke as kindly as I could while still getting the message across. "That there is not a dog to have for a pet, boys. Better you let him be. He's a good dog. Cares for me and the horses. Name's Wolf. Call him that because sometimes he acts like a wolf. Best you just let him be."

I watered and staked out the horses and then unsaddled. I piled the panniers against a willow bush a ways from the fire and wagon but close to the creek where there was a bit of sand to soften my night's sleep. Walking towards the fire with my tin mug in my hand, I asked, "Is that coffee I smell?"

Mrs. Ransom smiled and gestured with her chin, her hands full with a carving knife and a sizable cut of venison. "Help yourself. That's one thing we have a plenty of. It's meat we were running short of. Thanks for the venison.

You men ease back for a bit and keep the kids out of my way and we'll have dinner shortly."

Ransom and I were cautious at first, him still cradling the carbine and watching every move I made. For my part, I had sized these up as good folks but the gold on my packhorses would tempt a saint. I had no intention of talking about my summer's diggings. But we couldn't just sit there so I glanced over at Ransom and said, "You folks going on to Denver?"

"Denver for a small piece of business and then up north a ways."

Mrs. Ransom was close enough to join the conversation. She seemed to be much more talkative that her husband. "We're going to visit my husband's folks, Mr. Gates. They ranch in the north part of the state. The kids don't know their grandparents so we thought it was time."

"Good to have family," I said. "My folks are gone and I've lost track of my brothers and sister. I think about them from time to time."

The meal was good. We ate in silence which was the custom in most of the West with only the kids making a bit of talk. As soon as the cooking was done, Ransom carried a pail of water from the creek and put out the fire. He wasn't a talking man but he managed to say, "No smoke or reflected light. We should be alright until morning."

I nodded my agreement and continued sipping my coffee.

We spent a quiet evening and everyone went to their bedrolls at the first sign of evening's shadow. I didn't get much sleep and I suspect Ransom didn't either, both of us caring for our own matters. I got up once and prowled around some, checking the horses and taking a drink from the creek. I was lying with my eyes open when I watched Ransom make the same prowling circuit that I had made.

Morning came early with both the Ransoms and I loading up our gear and readying horses. Ransom didn't light a fire until full light and then he used dry sticks, building a mostly smokeless fire just big enough for the griddle and the coffeepot. I like a cautious man.

It took some work to get the Ransom's wagon down the creek and onto the Denver trail but we were soon lined out east. Ransom was riding his horse this morning with his wife handling the team. He stepped his horse over beside me and said, "That team and wagon don't make much time. We won't take it badly if you ride on ahead."

I patted Sam on the neck and grinned over at Ransom. "You look at this animal, Hank, you see a good, solid, faithful horse but he ain't much for speed. The packhorses pretty much prefer a slower pace, too. We'll tag along with you if that suits."

Ransom just nodded and kept riding.

When we stopped for lunch and to rest the horses, Mrs. Ransom asked, "Will you be spending the winter in Denver, Mr. Gates?"

I tipped my hat further back on my head and looked over at her. "No, I intend to look for a ranch to buy. And then I left a lady up in Miles City. Up Montana way. I didn't know it at the time but leaving her was a mistake. I'm going to go find her, hoping she's not married to someone else by now."

Mrs. Ransom looked over at her husband. "It's good ranching country up where your folks are, isn't it, Hank?"

That led to a discussion of land and cattle and horses that put some life into Ransom's voice as he described the beauty of the Front Range and the rolling hills around that area.

In Denver, I exchanged my gold for cash dollars and opened a bank account to hold it in, keeping out enough for traveling money. What Ransom called his small piece of business was also at a bank where he closed out an account that held a considerable sum from his previous horse-trading days.

I sold my extra packhorse and made some trail purchases. The Ransom family did a bit of shopping and then together we went to see some of the sights of the big city.

Within a few days, we were riding together into the little town of Canyon View. Ransom pointed over at the bank and said, "I expect if there's any land for sale the banker will know about it. Pa's ranch is twenty-five miles south on this other road. Calls it the C/R. You find yourself out that way, there'll be a welcome for you. Luck to you." He held out his hand for the first time.

I took his hand. My big hand felt small inside his oversized mitt. "Luck to y'all, too." I lifted my hat to Mrs. Ransom. "Glad to have met you folks and thanks for the meals."

They drove off to the hotel for the night and I rode to the hitch rail in front of the bank.

14

DORA

I LEFT Miles City after a short stay and joined up with a group of families who were traveling by wagon to Cheyenne.

The work at Potter's little newspaper started out well enough but within a couple of weeks, I had commitments for advertisements from nearly everyone in town. Except for some typesetting which Potter could do for himself, what I had done was work myself out of a job. But Potter kept me on for the full of the month and paid me the fifty dollars I'd asked for.

I found myself longing for a larger town with more prospects for a spinster lady, both financially and personally. So I squared my account with Mrs. O'Malley, said goodbye to the few folks I had met over my weeks in Miles City, and saddled my horse. She hated to leave the corral where she had been getting fat and lazy but within a couple of days, she was as anxious as I was to be moving along the trail.

A couple of times I turned my head to see if Wolf was following along. I was going to have to stop doing that.

I had thought often of Mr. Gates, wondering where he was and if he had filled those buckets with gold nuggets yet. There was a time or two that I wondered why I hadn't gone with him. Digging for gold held a certain exciting attraction and certainly I was never going to become financially secure working for wages in Miles City.

But then, in my more rational moments, I knew that going to the mountains for the summer with a man who wasn't my husband was not something I was prepared to do.

In Cheyenne, I landed a clerking job at a large ranch supply store. On a rainy, miserable fall day with a store full of customers making winter-ready purchases, I heard a familiar voice one aisle over say to another clerk, "I need a new rain slicker and enough grub to get me to Miles City; some jerky, a few cans of peaches, side of bacon, a few other things."

Smiling to myself, I stepped around the end of the counter and there stood Mr. Gates, big and handsome and determined-looking. I was surprised to say the least. But was it surprise that caused me to catch my breath and feel a tightening in my chest or was it something else?

I hesitated a bit and then said, "Why, what in all the world would make you want to travel all the way to Miles City, Mr. Gates? This is a poor time of year to be making a trip of that sort."

Mr. Gates whirled around so fast I was afraid he would bowl over the clerk or knock merchandise off the counter.

He was slow to respond to my question but then he pulled off his hat, combed his hair with his fingers and grinned his infectious grin. "Why, Dora. I was going to Miles City to find you but now it looks like I won't have to do that. You've cost this store some trade. Seems I won't need any trail supplies after all."

We were grinning at each other like two kids. "Why would you want to ride all that way to find me, Mr. Gates? Seems like a lot of riding for such a small reward."

Mr. Gates looked around him but everyone else seemed to be trying hard to appear as if they weren't listening.

"I had to come find you because it occurred to me that you have never told me your last name. Just Dora is all you ever said."

"And why does my last name matter, Mr. Gates?"

"Because I got wondering, laying in my tent on all those rainy nights up on that Colorado mountain, if you were really attached to your last name or not, and if perhaps you'd ever given any thought to changing it."

Now there were folks listening. In fact, clerks and customers alike had stopped what they were doing and were watching and listening. Some were smiling a bit.

"My last name is Bowman, Mr. Gates. It's a perfectly adequate name and one I've had all my life. But if I was to think about changing it, what do you think I should change it to?"

Mr. Gates looked around at the listening audience and seemed to take a deep breath, fighting down his embarrassment. Finally, he said, "Why, I was going to suggest that you change it to Gates. That is, if you don't have other immediate plans."

The thought of being Dora Gates scared me a bit having seen the various moods and actions of Mr. Gates, and sometimes marveling at his strength and vitality. But I have always been ready for a challenge so I tried to look very serious. "What exactly are you suggesting, Mr. Gates?"

I thought he might twist the brim right off his hat before he managed to say, "What I'm suggesting is that you might have missed me these past few months as much as I've missed you and that you might be favorable to the idea of marriage."

Remembering the mess Silas and I had made of a similar moment, I was careful with my words, "I have always been favorable to the idea of marriage, Mr. Gates. It was only a matter of finding a man who loved me and who I could love in return."

Mr. Gates put his hat back on and reached for my two hands. "Well, Dora, I surely do love you and perhaps over time you could learn to at least tolerate me and my clumsy ways."

I gave his hands a squeeze and said, "I believe I could do a lot more than merely tolerate you, Mr. Gates. Yes. If you want a straight answer, yes, I would very much like to become Mrs. Gates."

He pulled me into a fierce hug that nearly crushed my ribs while the customers cheered and clapped.

When the noise settled out, a voice said, "Now I suppose I'm going to have to find a replacement for the best clerk I ever hired." That brought on more laughter.

I looked over at the store owner and said, "I very much appreciate the job, Mr. Ambrewster, but I do believe I might have a better offer."

15

NOAH

WHEN I HEARD Dora's familiar voice in that ranch supply store I could hardly believe my ears. And when she greeted me with a smile and then a bit later agreed to be my wife, I felt like I could jump right over one of those there Rocky Mountains. No one has ever seriously accused me of being emotional but I'll admit to a bit of excitement right at that moment.

She took off her clerk's apron and we made our way through the wind-whipped rain outside. In the hotel dining room, I shook the rain off my Stetson and helped Dora out of her coat. The waiter took both our coats to hang up and said, "Sit anywhere you wish, folks, and I'll be right with you."

It was early for supper but the waiter said he'd see if the cook could find a couple of steaks and maybe some fried potatoes. He brought me coffee and a pot of tea for Dora. It seemed she preferred tea except in the mornings. She said coffee helped her to wake up early and stopped her from shooting folks, or coffeepots and such. We shared a small smile at that thought.

We sat there in silence, a little embarrassed, looking at each other. I really didn't have any idea what came next in this ritual we had entered into. Men and women had been doing this since time began. It would seem reasonable that there would be some rules laid out. But if there were, I had never heard about them.

So, like I usually do, I just barged in, "Do you know what you have just agreed to? You agreed to hitch yourself permanently to a man you hardly know and you haven't even asked where we might live or how we might manage to make our living and feed ourselves."

She returned my smile. "I expect you're going to tell me all in good time. I can still back out of this deal if I don't like what I hear." She didn't look too serious as she said it.

I leaned over the dining room table and looked very seriously at her. "You can't back out now. Not after all my long summer's planning and all the miles I've ridden and the further distance I was prepared to ride to Miles City and back, plus the embarrassment I just put myself through in that store. No, you can't back out now."

She shrugged and raised one eyebrow at me. "So, tell me. Are we to live in a sod-roofed dugout and eat squirrel stew?"

I chuckled a bit at that image and answered, "Well, I've done both and am not the worse off for either one but you're not that lucky. You're going to have to put up with a fine log house nestled just below the brow of a small hilltop overlooking several miles of green pasture. There's running streams and bits of forest here and there with the Eastern Slope Mountains of the Front Range off to the west.

"And we're going to have horses. Lots of horses."

She put her elbows on the table and leaned toward me. We were close enough to kiss which, for a moment, I thought might be a fine idea. The thought was interrupted by another question.

"What have you gone and done, Mr. Gates, or is it now appropriate and proper to call you Noah?

"Since you deserve a straight answer, I'll tell you; I've bought a ranch. The most beautiful ranch in the most beautiful country you will ever lay eyes on. We're going to have a horse ranch just south of Canyon View, Colorado. You're going to love it there."

"Am I really? Well, you might be right at that, Noah. I told you once how much I loved living on the farm and you told me how much you loved horses so I imagine we will be able to work it all out provided we can find an agreement on what morning looks like. You know, daylight and all. When do I get to see this wonderful ranch of yours?"

It was the first time she had used my given name. It sounded good coming off her lips. But I had to correct her, "It's not my ranch, Dora; it's our ranch, yours and mine. I thought of it that way when I bought it. I thought of you with every ounce of gold I broke out of those rocks; the gold that paid for our ranch. There was no part of the past few months that didn't include you somewhere in my mind.

"After completing a deal for the ranch and all the furniture left in the house and the few horses still running in the pasture, I sat in a rocker on the veranda and looked over the valley running away behind the barn and corrals. That valley and those hills run all the way to the Front Range. I doubt as how I'll ever get tired of looking at it.

"Anyway, I sat there rocking and imagined you sitting

in the other rocker. Then I saddled up and headed for Miles City. Sure glad I didn't miss you in Cheyenne."

"I'm glad, too. So how far is it to this ranch?"

We were still sitting with our faces almost touching across the round table. Temptation was about to get the better of me so I leaned back in my chair. "It's just one long day's ride away. If we were to be ready to ride at first light tomorrow, we could be there by evening; a little tired maybe but we'd be there. Or we could put it off a day or two if you wanted to get married here in Cheyenne."

"No, I would prefer to get married in what is to be our hometown. I assume this Canyon View has a church and a minister who can marry us.

"But that brings up something we really need to discuss, Noah. I come from a believing and church-going family, and have attended myself as opportunity allowed although those opportunities in this unsettled west are fewer than they were back home. But I intend to take advantage of whatever worship opportunities are available.

"What is your spiritual background, Noah?"

Well, that one caught me by surprise. I hesitated a few moments looking at Dora and finally said, "Church is not a subject I'm given to putting a lot of thought into, Dora. It's not that I'm not a believer or that I've never been to meeting. It's just that somehow I always found something else to do come that time of a Sunday morning. Seems there's always more work to do than hours to do it in.

"I know a fair bit about horses and a little about cattle. I can talk range conditions with the best of them and when I study the sky I can do a fair country job of predicting the weather.

"But I never read much more than a few storybooks I carried in my saddlebags. Nothing serious or studied out that might make a far-riding man think about things that really matter."

"Tell me what you've read, Noah."

"About the most serious reading I ever did was by that fellow that was traipsing around the west some years back. Mark Twain he calls himself although I've heard that's not his real name. He writes interesting stories and I've spent many an evening bent over the light of a campfire reading them but no one would call them any more than just a story.

"I had a Bible once but somehow I couldn't get my tongue or my mind, either one, wrapped around all those big words."

Dora leaned back in her chair while the waiter placed our orders on the table, then smiled just a small smile.

"That will have to do for now. At least it's something we can work on. And you're not alone in having trouble with the big words."

I realized later how much I still had to learn. When a woman tells you that it's something we can work on, she has an entirely different meaning than what a man would at first understand.

We ate in silence for a while before she looked at me with a bit of a mischievous grin as if she was poking me with a stick to see what I would do. "What became of your Bible?"

I set my fork and knife down on the plate and leaned back. "I'd be a bit embarrassed to have to tell that story, Dora."

Dora clapped her hands in front of her and smiled from ear to ear. "Oh, I have to hear it. You seem to be good at everything you do. I'd love to hear the other side."

I pushed some steak across my plate and studied her. As far as I could tell she wasn't going to back down so I started in, "The sad truth is, I fell off my horse. Hadn't done that since I was knee-high."

Dora laughed right out loud and said, "Now I really have to hear this. I can't picture you falling off a horse."

I closed my eyes and shook my head a bit remembering. "Well, it was like this. One cold winter day, my horse and I were trying to get across a small coulee. The bank was pretty steep but, all in all, it looked doable enough. But the snow was deeper than I thought and my horse's movements started a small avalanche. He lost his footing and his front legs folded under him. His nose hit the snow first and then he went right over in a tumble. We ended up going head over heels down that steep, snow-covered side hill. I flew off on his first stumble.

"When we finally came to a stop at the bottom of the slope, I had a broken arm and my saddlebags had flown open scattering my collection of treasures all over a brush and snow-filled ravine.

"I dug all around in the snow but I never did find that Bible or the tintype of my folks that I had carried for years.

"I never did read that Bible much and never had once since so you can see that my education is a little lacking on the subject."

Dora laughed and then put her hand over her mouth. "Oh, my. I don't mean to laugh at your broken arm or your loss. I was just picturing you and the horse and the snow. You must have made quite a sight."

"I suppose we did but my arm was hurting so bad I didn't think much about how it all looked."

I figured Dora might as well hear it all so's we wouldn't have to talk any more about it.

"My parents were church-going folks. And if it's important to you, I'll pull a razor across my face and take a bath on Saturday night and put on a clean shirt for Sunday morning.

"But don't ask me to sing. There's not one person in the whole world desperate enough for music that they would want to hear me sing. Cattle have been known to beg for mercy and run for cover when I sang to them on the trail."

Dora continued with, "I'm glad to hear about the Saturday night bath and shave, Noah, but I'm thinking you may wish to repeat that effort more than just on Saturdays."

Like I said, I had so much still to learn.

NOAH

WE WERE silent for a while with the slight clicking of knife and fork on the white porcelain plates the only sound.

After a bit, I put down my fork. The waiter silently took our plates away and replaced them with smaller plates of apple pie. Neither of us really noticed what he was doing.

I reached into my big jacket pocket. I pulled out a sample of my summer's work and laid it on the table.

Dora gasped and stared at it. Finally she picked it up, turning it every which way, as if to see if it was real. "Is this what I think it is?"

"That, Mrs. Gates-to-be, is quartz. And those jagged chunks sticking out all over it are gold. That there one piece is worth probably several months' wages for a hard-working cowhand or a clerk in a ranch supply store."

She caressed the rock like something out of a fantasy. "It's beautiful and wonderful and it near takes my breath away. Is this the only piece you found or was there more?"

"There was more. A lot more. Most of it I broke out of the quartz to lighten the load down the mountain. Would've needed three or four pack animals to get that quartz out to a mill so I took the easy stuff and left the rest lay there. Someone will come along some day and pocket my leavings.

"But I got the bigger pieces of gold. Mighty hard work, breaking up that quartz, and I had no way to sift out the fine gold. I came near wearing the skin off my fingers picking through those sharp rock pieces. Someone with a bit of equipment and some know-how could work over the pile of rock I left up there and fill some pouches with good color.

"I turned my leather pouches into spendable currency at a bank down in Denver. After paying for the ranch, there's a deposit in that bank that still has enough left in it for a good stallion and a small herd of mares. Might pick up a few breeding heifers, too. I kept just a few larger pieces like this. I enjoy looking at them."

Dora turned the quartz over and over in her hands for another few moments. "Sometimes I wonder at you, Mr. Gates. You seem to take things in stride with no feeling of wonderment. I remember you putting those two thieves down in the mud and pretending to shoot them, and then coming for supper in the cafe as if nothing had ever happened.

"And now you're showing me enough gold to excite most men into a frenzy and you're acting like it's nothing at all. I do really wonder about you."

I picked up the rock when she laid it on the table. I let a full minute go by while I turned the rock around in my hands. I hadn't told her about killing the Sommers brothers up on that mountain and didn't want to bring it up now. The thing she was mistaken on was that I wasn't near as easy about the happenings she mentioned as she thought I was.

I didn't enjoy fighting and had never killed a man before being challenged by the Sommers. I took the doing of it hard, no matter that they were thieving low-lifes who were trying to kill me at the time. But I couldn't see as how talking about it would ease my thoughts so I kept quiet.

Then I glanced up and pointed at her with the rock. "What excites me is the fact that you've agreed to be my wife. I'm very thankful for the gold I found this summer but it would mean nothing at all if I had to spend it alone."

Dora reached over and caressed the top of my hand, saying nothing.

I turned my hand over and gripped her fingers while I laid the rock in the center of the table with my other hand.

"What I thought we'd do, Dora, is have a jeweler melt this gold down and turn it into a wedding band for you. But I wanted you to see the rock it came from before melting it out."

Dora picked up the rock and, clutching it in her two hands, held it to her chest. "I wouldn't hear tell of such a thing. To melt down something of this beauty would be a terrible thing to do. Anyway, this is far too much gold for a single ring. We'll buy a ring or figure something else out."

I just shrugged, again seeing how much my thinking differed from hers.

When I pulled the saddled horses up before the hotel the next morning, Dora was already in the cafe waiting for me. She was dressed in her riding clothes and had left two carpetbags beside the hotel door. The slight rim of hazy light off to the east said it was still a half-hour short of full daylight. The fact she was up and ready told me something although I wasn't exactly sure just what it was.

Dora didn't do early mornings well and remembering

that she had her pistol, I'd ridden up to the hotel prepared to sit on the veranda and wait her out. But there she sat looking prim and proper and ready for the day. I said not a word beyond 'good morning' lest I found myself facing trouble. I took a seat and ordered breakfast.

Folks were moving about and some of the stores were opening up. We ate and paid the cook to put a lunch together for us. By shortly after first light, we were on our way, bundled up in warm clothing for the feel of fall was in the air. Anyway, this country is all six- and seven-thousand feet high and higher in places. A cold wind can be expected almost anytime at that elevation.

Dora had been wearing men's pants and shirts on her ride from Dakota but on this day she had on a split skirt, something I had only ever seen a few times before. When I first saw her in what looked like an ordinary skirt, I thought she might ask for a sidesaddle but she swung easily into her own saddle, settled the skirt around her and kicked her horse into motion.

I watched and said nothing which I judged to be the safest thing to say right at that moment.

As we were crossing the Union Pacific tracks on our way out of Cheyenne, a night train pulled up to a chuffing stop on a siding a little ways from the station. Boxcar doors flew open and loading ramps were lowered into place. Blue-clad troopers started leading horses down the ramps while other troops lined up in formation a short ways away and a gravel-voiced sergeant shouted orders. One thing the army did well was get up in the morning.

I was tempted to ride over and take a look at some brands but I let it go. Turns out that was a mistake. Or perhaps not, given that my mind was full of Dora and the starting of our life together.

It was a long ride on a cool, fall day but by late evening

Dora was asleep in her hotel room in Canyon View and I was working over the horses at the livery stable. After a single drink at the saloon, I made my way to my own room and fell into bed exhausted.

The next morning, we rode out to the ranch, a short ten-mile ride. Dora started off the day chattering like a bird that had found a nest already built. But as we drew closer to the ranch, she fell silent. I glanced at her from time to time to try to read her thoughts but got nowhere at all for my efforts.

Finally I spoke up, "You're quiet this morning. Having doubts about becoming Mrs. Gates?"

Dora smiled just a small smile at me. "No doubts at all on that matter, Mr. Gates. I'm just finding the idea of having a home again and putting my feet under my own table a bit overwhelming, almost as overwhelming as those magnificent glacier-topped mountains off to the west. I've never seen their like. And then I can't help wonder what this ranch and the log house are like. You've built it up some and I don't want to be disappointed."

We were approaching a slight rise in the road that was preventing us from seeing ahead. I waited just a few moments and then as we came to the top of the rise, I nodded off to the west. "You don't have to wonder any longer, Mrs. Gates-to-be. There's your home and your ranch."

Dora gasped and pulled her horse to a stop. She sat still as a statue. The silence dragged on for an uncomfortable length of time until I was wondering if it was only me that saw the beauty of the place and if she was fighting disappointment.

The ranch headquarters lay in a bit of a basin with the ranch yard itself mostly level and the lands behind the house showing a slight rise to the north; not much but enough to stop most of the winter winds. The roof line was long and low with two large dormers showing where the upstairs bedrooms were.

A covered veranda ran along the entire front, raised just two steps above the ground level. The veranda faced south and west but mostly south. From the veranda rocking chairs, a body could watch the sun rise or set, either one. A smaller covered porch outside the kitchen door faced mostly north and east.

The view of the mountains was worth the sitting with another cup of coffee in the evening to my way of seeing things. Hopefully, Dora would come to an agreement on that. The log walls of the house and barn had been allowed to grow silver as the sun, rain and wind did their weathering year by year. The window and door trims and the gingerbread along the eves were all painted white. The roof was painted red as were the roofs of the barn and all the outbuildings.

As we watched, five white-tailed deer came from behind the bunkhouse and started browsing among the trees and shrubs.

There was a fenced-off garden yard and numerous trees planted around the house blocking the sweltering summer sun but also some of the view of the yard. The trees showed less than ten years of growth so I suspected they had been planted after most of the risk of Indian raids had been put behind the country.

A small stream ran five-feet wide down the south side of the yard carrying irrigation water to the garden and relief to thirsty livestock, then moving on to water the pasture land below. All in all, I found it a pleasant and well laid-out ranch. I was counting on Dora to feel the same but her silence was beginning to concern me.

Finally, Dora reached over and took my hand. Looking

at her I could see there were tears in her eyes. I thought she was unhappy but it turns out I was wrong again. Seems that was destined to happen a lot.

"Mr. Gates, I have never seen anything so wonderful. I know you didn't build the place with your own hands but you chose it and that tells me a lot. The builder had an eye for beauty and so do you even if you don't know it. We can ride on down in a bit but right now I just want to look at it, soak it in, kind of."

We stared off together at the house and barns, the bunkhouse and smaller outbuildings, and the corrals.

The stream that flowed down the side of the yard seemed to set off the miles of browning grass that would green up again in the spring.

Stretching off into the distance, the uplift of hillsides and forest edged and pointed the way towards the Front Range.

The few horses that came with the place were grazing close to the barn and, in the distance, we could see the smoke of a neighbor's breakfast fire.

Finally, Dora asked, "How in the world did you find this beautiful ranch? Canyon View is a pretty out-of-the-way town. What caused you to ride this way?"

"Met a family riding up from the gold fields. Rode along with them for company and mutual protection. They were riding to visit his folks who ranch south of here. They spoke so highly of the country that I rode along just to take a look. The banker pointed me at this place and I grabbed it up before someone else put their brand on it."

Dora listened quietly and then without another word kicked her horse into a slow walk. Riding side by side, we made our way down the grade and along the two-track wagon road. The road followed the easiest path around and through the hills until it ended up west of the ranch.

Our ranch would have land on both sides of the trail. The hills here were mostly grass-covered with sizable patches of forest dotting their tops.

We rode through the log gate posts and up to the ranch yard. Before leaving for Miles City, I had taken time to burn the G-bar brand into the gate posts. As I pointed the brands out to Dora, I explained that I had used that brand back in Indian Territory. All my animals had carried it and I intended to stick with it.

Dora had been handling her own horse just fine without my help all the way from Dakota Territory but as we pulled up in front of the house, she held out her hand and said, "Hand me down, Noah."

I guess she saw something special in her first arrival at her new home. I helped her down and kept holding her hand as we climbed the steps to the veranda. Once on the veranda, she stopped and turned around, again taking in the details of the ranch yard.

Without a word, she moved towards the front door.

I reached and opened the door and took her by the elbow as we walked into the house. I had purchased the place fully furnished so it looked just like it had over all the long years since it was built. Inside the house, Dora stepped away from me and started to slowly walk into the big living room.

I turned and went back outside. I sat down on the rocker I had been sitting on when I decided I had to find Dora in Miles City, or wherever she was.

Dora seemed to be a long time in the house but that was alright with me. I had nowhere else to go anyway. I planned on spending a good many years sitting right on that veranda, enjoying the cool of an evening after my work was done. So I took being there as good practice for the future.

DORA

SOMEONE HAD PUT a lot of planning and care into the building and furnishing of the ranch house. It was well thought out with wide doorways and a sturdy bench at the entrance, a row of wooden pegs along the wall for hanging winter coats on. The furnishings I could see from the doorway were appropriate to a working ranch. The floors glistened with well-oiled hardwood and the couch and chairs were hardy and comfortable.

The kitchen range was large enough to cook for a crew although, with the bunkhouse and its attached cookhouse, it's doubtful if it had been used that way for some time.

I climbed the stairs. There were four bedrooms, all furnished. I took just a quick look at the master room and then stepped down the hallway towards the smaller rooms. I assumed that these had been for the children. They were similar in size with sloped ceilings and a small windowed dormer in each. The furnishings were simple but adequate.

The bulky quilts folded at the foot of each bed were an indication that these rooms could be cool on a blustery winter night.

I then returned for a much longer look at the master bedroom. There was a big four-poster bed covered with handmade quilts. A couple of fluffed-up pillows lay against the headboard. A large oak armoire with two mirrored doors stood against one wall. A long oak table held its place below a large dormer window which faced south. In the center of the table stood a spectacular Aladdin oil lamp, a fine example of the best in glass craftsmanship.

A beautifully upholstered, oak-frame rocking chair sat beside a smaller table which still had a book lying open on it.

It was a large and comfortable room. I would guess it was a room the lady of the house had spent much time in.

I was impressed that the gentleman who had owned the place had left it looking as if he and his wife had just stepped out for a few minutes and would soon return. It was sobering to know that the lady was gone forever and the husband was now unable to care for the ranch or himself.

It was a very welcoming space and I found myself anxious to make it my own.

As I looked at the four-poster bed, my mind started to wander thinking of Mr. Gates, marriage and my becoming Mrs. Gates. All of the unknowns both frightened and excited me. I felt a strange feeling run through me and I felt myself blushing.

I'm not sure if it was the fright or the excitement that made me turn and quickly step out of the room, making my way down the stairs and out to the veranda.

I was just in time to see a stunningly beautiful girl walking towards us from the bunkhouse. She waved and hollered, "Welcome back, Noah. I didn't expect to see you here this soon. Did you find her already or decide to give it up?" There was no shyness in her at all; it was as if she was familiar with talking to and dealing with men and took it as a natural occurrence.

It seems that about that time she noticed me standing in the doorway.

"Well, hello there. I didn't see you at first. I'm Laura. You must be Mrs. Gates. Noah said he was off to find the most beautiful and wonderful lady he had ever met and it looks like he got the job done. Welcome to your new home."

I suppose I stood somewhere around average in looks but no one had ever called me beautiful. Pleasant-looking is about the best I'd ever heard. One fellow called me comfortable-looking whatever that was supposed to mean. But to hear that Noah had said that about me was gratifying even if it was a shameful exaggeration.

Noah jumped to his feet to introduce us. "Dora, this is Laura. She and her family live down the way a bit. I stopped into their ranch some time back hoping to get one of Laura's brothers to take care of the place while I was away looking for you but none of the boys could be spared from the work. Laura offered and I took her up on it. Couldn't leave the place empty.

"Laura, this is Dora but she's not Mrs. Gates yet. I'm hoping to change that right soon now."

We said our 'hellos' and Laura went to make coffee. She was clearly more comfortable in my new home than I was but I figured I could deal with that when the time came.

We visited for a while before heading back to town.

We rode along quietly until curiosity finally got the better of me. "What's the story on Laura?" I asked.

Noah glanced my way and shrugged. "I have no real

idea. I'm new to this country same as you are and I don't know the folks about. I just rode into her Pa's ranch yard and introduced myself saying I was looking for someone to watch over the place and feed the stock while I was gone. Looked like a ne'er-do-well outfit to me once I got right into the yard, raising more kids than cattle as the saying is, but that might not be a fair judgment.

"Didn't hear a first name but the family name is Abner. Apparently moved in from Kentucky a few years back. Took to the hills with their ranch. Those rolling hills off to the west seem to go on and on, right up to the Rockies. Maybe they remind Abner of his home. Too hilly for me.

"Anyway, when her father said he couldn't spare any of the boys, Laura offered and the place looks fine so I guess she had no problems."

"She's very beautiful."

Noah turned on his exasperating grin. "She is. She'll turn some heads if she ever gets free of that run-down ranch. But it don't matter to me since I've got you."

I decided that no further comment was required.

We rode into town and right up to the hitch rail beside the church. A man was just coming out of the side door.

Noah nodded towards the man who was closing the church door. "I would guess that's your man."

Not to put too fine a point on it but I rather thought of him as our man; that is if this marriage was to involve two people and I rather believed that it should. I didn't push the thought though. I had fought some foolish battles in the past, mainly on principle, and I had noticed that even when I won, I lost. So I stepped off my horse and passed the reins to Noah before speaking, "Would you be the minister of this church, sir?"

The man lifted his hat and held it in front of him like a

shield. "Rev. Josiah Brockton at your service. What can I do for you folks?"

Noah had tied the horses and stepped up beside me.

"We're of a mind to get married and since this is the only church we've seen in town, we thought to inquire about having you say the words."

The reverend flashed a large, friendly smile and nodded his head. "Nothing would give me more pleasure. Folks around here mostly just call me Josiah. Perhaps you would be good enough to tell me your names and a bit about yourselves.

"In fact, I am just about to walk home for lunch. I live right over there." He pointed with his hat. "Come meet my wife and we'll have a visit and a bite to eat."

I looked a question over at Noah and received a hunched shoulder in response. The reverend looked like a cowboy who was taken off the range and had gotten himself stuck in town. I am sure that eased the questions running through Noah's mind.

I couldn't imagine the reverend spending much time drinking tea with the ladies, his big hands trying to hold a dainty tea cup with his fingers unable to get a grip on the handle.

We walked with him to the house. The introductions were made and we offered the obligatory compliments on the house, the town, the delightful odors wafting from the big coal stove in the kitchen, and the baby sleeping in the homemade cradle. Mrs. Brockton said, "We so seldom have company. Most folks around here work long hours and have little time for a leisurely lunch. Please take a seat at the table. I hope you don't mind chicken soup and bread. The bread is just out of the oven so it's fresh if nothing else. And Josiah churned butter for us just a couple of days ago. I hope you are not in a hurry. I would look forward to a visit."

As the reverend had requested, we outlined our situation. At a couple of points during the telling, the good pastor raised an eyebrow, mostly when I told about Noah being hired as a guide in Dakota and of us traveling so many miles together. It rankled me just a bit, thinking that raised eyebrow was casting doubt on my morals just like Silas had done. Even understanding the proprieties that were running around in his head didn't make me any happier.

"Don't you be reading anything into that that isn't there in reality, Reverend Brockton."

That caught him just a bit off guard, him not realizing that I had noticed his changed expression or the raised eyebrow. He blushed a bit, cleared his throat unnecessarily, and said, "My most sincere apologies, Dora and Noah. I meant no offense. But you will, I am sure, understand that the gossip hounds will make great sport out of that story. It might be best to not repeat it and you can rest assured that it is safe with us. Please go on with the story."

I finished up by telling about how Noah had purchased the ranch after his summer in the Colorado high country and of his startling me with that beautiful gold-laden rock.

Rev. Brockton interrupted with a smile. "That's the old Hampton place. We all knew someone had purchased it but we had no idea who it was. That's a great choice, Noah. There's not many places to compare for beauty. The land is good, too. The only reason one of the neighbors didn't pick it up for the land alone was that Hampton insisted it be kept as a ranching unit. He didn't want to see the house and barn fall to disuse.

"Mrs. Hampton died last year and Hampton developed heart trouble so he lives here in town now with a daughter and her family. They own the abattoir and butcher shop in town. You'd have a friend for life if you were to invite him to come and visit the old place from time to time."

Our time together and the conversation moved along, sliding easily from subject to subject. The afternoon moved along, too. It seemed there was nothing pressing at the little church that demanded the pastor's immediate attention. Mrs. Brockton put another pot of coffee on for the men and a pot of tea for the two of us.

Finally, Rev. Brockton got back to the subject of the wedding. "When and where would you like to have this wedding, folks?"

Noah had said very little during the visit but now I looked to him for a comment. He lifted his coffee cup and took a big swallow, then looked around the table. "How about right now, right here. Seems simple enough. How hard can it be?"

Mrs. Brockton broke out in gales of laughter while the reverend leaned back in his chair with a wide smile after giving Noah a conspiratorial slap on the shoulder.

When Mrs. Brockton more or less got hold of herself again, she studied Noah for a moment and said, "You're priceless, Mr. Gates, simply priceless." Then she again broke out in laughter.

Noah looked a little bit lost as if he wasn't quite sure what was happening.

When a degree of decorum returned to the little kitchen, the reverend talked directly to me, "While I fully understand Noah's position on this, the final decision might be more in your area, Dora. May I make a suggestion?"

At our silence, he carried on, "You have purchased a stunningly beautiful home. I could think of no better place for a wedding and I know your neighbors would welcome the opportunity to meet you and join in the celebrations. If we were to arrange everything for Sunday afternoon the week after next at your ranch home, there would be enough time to get the news out and folks would come from miles around. There is little enough happening in any ranching country that people look for opportunities to get together.

"And, of course, we would announce the date at church. You have to meet your neighbors sooner or later so why not do it up in royal style? Your wedding would be the social event of the year."

And so it was decided. But in that deciding I seemed to lose control, giving way to Mrs. Rev. Brockton who was clearly looking forward to doing something more challenging than making meals at home and smiling on Sunday mornings.

18

NOAH

So, we had the full of a week plus a couple of days to wait. Wait and make wedding arrangements. It seemed the one thing that wasn't needed in all of this was my advice. The whole thing looked like a clear exaggeration of needs to me but I had to admit that I had no knowledge at all on the matter of marriages and how they were put together. The ladies had their way with no obvious objections from me.

Dora said she would book her hotel room for the full week while I suggested that it would be best if I stayed at the ranch to care for it and the few horses I kept there. Dora would hear nothing of the sort. I couldn't understand that.

The Rev. Brockton didn't help any at all. "You've been gone to Cheyenne for a while, Noah. Who's been caring for the ranch while you were away?"

Dora didn't give me an opportunity to answer. "A young neighbor girl named Laura. She seems quite nice but we really don't know anything about her or her family."

Why her family should matter I didn't understand but the minister raised his eyebrows again and gave me a questioning look while his wife reached over and patted Dora's hand. Clearly I was outnumbered here so again I didn't push it. I was starting to think that I had better stick to raising horses and hunting gold.

Rev. Brockton pursed his lips, gathering his thoughts and his words. Finally, he looked directly at me. "If I may make a suggestion just to quiet the wagging tongues, you understand, perhaps you should either terminate your employment of Laura and take care of the ranch yourself or spend the nights until the wedding here in town."

Figuring I needed a steady hand at the ranch until Dora and I could move in permanently, I chose to take a room at the hotel. I didn't like it but Dora explained to me how getting off to a good start was important in a new town.

Dora and I went to the little church on Sunday and met a few of the folks. Following the service Dora had such a crowd of ladies gathered around her, pushing and elbowing me aside in order to get closer to her, that I found myself standing alone on the edge of the chattering collection of women. I decided it would be easier to walk outside to wait. It seemed to me that all the women were talking at once. How anything helpful would come out of the avalanche of words was a mystery to me. But many things involving women and weddings were a mystery to me so I let it go. I didn't seem to be needed anyway.

A few of the men sauntered over and introduced themselves, giving a rough idea of where their ranches lay and generally welcoming us to the district. The news of the wedding didn't seem important enough for the men to push aside their continuing discussion of cattle prices and range conditions.

But the gaggle of women around Dora was all abuzz with questions and advice and eager nodding of heads and whispered comments along with more than just a few sly glances my way.

When the women finally managed to pull themselves away from Dora, the crowd in the wagon yard started to thin out. Dora walked over to where I was sitting on a wagon tongue flipping my Barlow knife into the grass like a kid playing mumblety-peg. I stood up and, with Dora's arm linked in mine, we turned toward the little town's main street.

Just about that time a man wearing a sheriff badge strolled up. I hadn't seen him in church but the woman walking beside him had been playing the pump organ. "Morning, sir." He held out his hand. "Walter Howard, Sheriff. And this is Mrs. Howard. You might've already met her. Plays the organ although I don't often get to hear it what with being busy keeping the town safe and all."

I couldn't see that keeping the little town safe would strain a grown man to where he couldn't take a Sunday morning off from duty but I said nothing. Seems I was getting familiar with saying nothing since coming to Canyon View.

"Like to meet the new folks as they come to town. How would you folks like to join us for lunch at the dining room? We usually go to the hotel for lunch on Sunday. Come join us."

I wasn't sure if he was offering a friendly invite or an official demand. I had no desire to use the lunch time to discuss the Sommers boys or stolen horses or anything else that I considered to be private. I had finally told Dora about the misadventure on the mountain and the burying of the two men. I didn't figure more talk would help anything. Dora didn't seem to question the invite to lunch though. "We'd love to."

I didn't get a say on the issue but we planned to eat somewhere so it didn't much matter where or who with. I finally decided that if the sheriff had formal business in mind he wouldn't trouble me with it in the dining room with the ladies present. And, anyway, that bit of trouble over in the mountains was many a mile outside his jurisdiction.

As we were sitting in the dining room, a troop of cavalry rode past almost filling the short business street of Canyon View. Even though the troops looked tired and were covered in dust, the lieutenant had them riding in order with their backs straight as rifle barrels and with all eyes forward.

They rode smartly past and with a shouted order from the sergeant which we could only slightly hear from the dining room, came to a halt beside the livery barn. At the order to dismount and stand down, the troopers stepped to the ground and led their animals into the shade on the north side of the barn. They loosened their saddle girths and took turns pumping water into the big trough until all the horses were cared for.

Any time I saw a group of horses I was tempted to search out their brands. But just as I had that same thought when I saw the troop unloading in Cheyenne, I let it pass.

The sheriff commented, "Wonder what that's all about. Can't hardly remember the last time we seen any soldier boys out this way."

We all let that comment pass and went on with our lunch.

19

NOAH

As I've already come out and admitted, my knowledge of how a wedding should be done is a little short of complete having somehow avoided any opportunity to be involved in such an affair up to this point in my life. What was planned to happen on the G-bar on that sunny fall afternoon seemed a little excessive to me. But Dora was happy and seemed to be smiling all the time so I let it be.

After church service let out on the appointed day, the women were excited and gushing over Dora while the kids were running every which way around the churchyard. The men were getting their rigs lined out and trying to look patient as they waited for their womenfolk to climb aboard. The kids were all mixed together riding wagons with their friends, their parents not knowing which wagon they were on.

There were pots and pans of food stacked in the back of

most buggies and it all looked more like the Fourth of July than a simple cow-country wedding.

The road from town to the G-bar looked like I imagined the exodus of the children of Israel must have looked leaving Egypt except there was no sign of Pharaoh's army chasing us. It seemed everyone from the church service and a bunch of others from town had their buggies or wagons packed with food and other foofaraw and were following one another down the dirt road.

I'd never seen so much celebrating since they hanged the Hanson brothers back in '68 down in Indian Territory where my folks had their small spread. I'm not exactly sure why I remembered that hanging on my wedding day but somehow every detail of it came back clear as if it was yesterday, even the fact that it was a cowboy-preacher who had taken center stage.

I had to keep reminding myself that getting married was my own idea.

When we got to the ranch, I helped Dora down from the buggy just as a no-longer young, busy-looking woman that we hadn't seen at church came over and said, "Dora, I'm Hanna Ransom. Just you take your ease. We'll look after everything and call you when it's time." With that she was gone in a huff of importance.

Dora turned and looked into my glazing-over eyes. "You have to remember, Mr. Gates, that getting married was your idea."

Did she somehow know that this very same thought had just rambled through my head?

She gave me a small smile that might have held some smugness or it might have been fear. I'm not just exactly sure which.

Just about that time, a bowlegged dried-up old cowboy limped over and shook my hand introducing himself as

Clark Ransom. His hand-strength was a contradiction to the worn-out appearance of his much-abused body and the cobweb of wrinkles and tracks across his face. Idly I wondered how he managed to shave all those creases. His multi-stained hat and his run-over boots suggested that he held his cows as being of more importance than his clothes or our wedding, either one.

"Good to meet a new neighbor, Noah. And you, too, Miss. Don't you be thinking too much about my missus and her pushy ways. There never was a dinner or a dance or a roundup that she didn't take control of. Brings me pleasure to see her doing it, knowing she's leaving me alone all the while.

"My son tells me you met along the trail and rode here with him. Good to have the boy home. I can use the help." He made no mention of his son's wife or their two boys.

Dora gave him a strange look and excused herself. I was a little stuck for words myself. Ransom thrust his jaw in the direction of a group of men down by the corral. "Come meet some of the boys. Might be your last chance for a while to talk uninterrupted."

I wasn't sure if he was making a joke or not so I didn't reply.

One by one the men stuck out their hands and offered their names and a rough description of where their spreads lay. First up was a pushy sort of man with a Texas drawl and a fancy opinion of himself. "Bob Stanton, Circle S, twelve miles out the east road from town. Fairly new here myself. Took a while to learn the ropes but it's a good country when you get right down to it."

I heard so many names they were all a jumble in my mind by the time it was done and, as I looked up, there were more folks coming down the lane. I knew I'd hear and forget their names, too.

The last man to step forward gave his name, "Hamilton Robb, H-R, eight miles out the Boulder Road. But the way the hills run, your G-bar and the H-R join for about a half-mile along the river. There's a little bridge and a gate in the fence where my wife used to ride over and visit Mrs. Hampton from time to time. Perhaps our wives can visit a bit too when opportunity allows."

I shook his hand and glanced back up to the house. "I'm sure Dora would like that but perhaps not for a week or two."

The men all burst out laughing and it took me a moment to figure out what they were laughing about.

One of the last wagons to arrive was Hank and Sarah Ransom and their two boys. I saw them pull their rig into the shade of the barn. They stepped down from the wagon but were obviously hesitating about joining the crowd. I walked over to them. "Good to see y'all. I haven't had the chance to thank you for guiding me to this country. Great country and a great ranch. I hope we'll be seeing a lot of you if you decide to stay. Come join the folks."

Sarah slipped her arm under Hank's elbow. "We might just as well Hank. We'll have to face them sooner or later."

I had no idea what she was talking about so, like I always seemed to do, I barged right in, "You'll know the old timers, Hank. I'm sure they'll be happy to see you again."

Hank gave me a troubled look. "I'm not totally sure of that, Noah. Something I never told you. I'm just released from prison. Been locked up for three years. Killed a man in a fistfight. Pa's okay with me having killed a man but he's having a hard time with his son being in prison. Seems a strange twisting of values but that's Pa. I don't know about the neighbors. They may not want me around."

I thought about that for a moment and in my imagination I saw the two Sommers boys lying crumpled and bleeding on the rocks. "That's the past, Hank. The other ranchers will be fine. Dora and I want you here. Come and say hello."

I took them to meet Dora first and left Sarah with the ladies. The kids shyly looked to where the other kids were playing. Then Hank and I walked together to the corral where the men were gathered. Hamilton Robb looked up at our approach and his face lit up in a smile. "Hank! Good to see you. I didn't know you were home. Welcome!" As they shook hands, the other men started gathering around.

I left them there and went to see if I could help Dora. I couldn't.

DORA

WHEN THAT BOWLEGGED, wizened old man hobbled over to say his name and shake Noah's hand, he turned his head sideways and spewed out a great gob of ugly brown juice before he could speak. I was fearful that it might kill off the yard grass.

"Clark Ransom," he said to Noah and then raised his battered and torn hat a bit to me.

I knew enough about ranchers to not judge them by first appearance; most families cleaned themselves up before coming to town. But I had seen men come into that Cheyenne supply store I worked in looking like they hadn't a dime to their names but who in fact were both land- and cattle-rich. I had learned not to judge.

Still, I made my exit from Mr. Ransom just as quickly as I thought polite although I'm not sure if politeness was even a factor in the old man's makeup.

By the time I struggled my way through the women and heard their names, I was ready for a bit of quiet. The kids were screaming and laughing and I gave some thought to suggesting they go play by the creek. Or perhaps in the creek. I don't know much about kids and this didn't seem like quite the right day to be learning.

I sought shelter in the house but it was more a beehive of activity than the yard was. I finally settled for a rocking chair on the veranda. In the second rocker sat a very attractive young lady nursing a baby. The baby was hidden discreetly under a light blanket. I introduced myself and asked her name.

"Wanda Robb. My husband Hamilton and I have the H-R, just over to the east a ways. The baby's name is William. William Johnson Robb. My husband tells me he's the image of the grandfather he's named after. I've never met Hamilton's parents so I take his word on that."

"Is this your first child?" I asked.

"Yes. Hamilton is hoping William is the first of many but I'm not quite so sure. He's a delight to have but the process, in the heat of summer, was not just exactly as I might have imagined."

She folded the blanket back and turned the baby for me to see. I looked and then smiled at her. "He's a beautiful little boy. I haven't met your husband but with your beauty I don't see how your babies could be anything but beautiful.

"I seem to see beautiful women everywhere I look here. It's almost like there's a committee that inspects women before they're allowed entry to the community."

Wanda laughed and leaned a little towards me. "I've never heard of any committee like that but if such a thing exists, I suspect it has something to do with the group that

meets in the saloon on Saturday evenings. They call themselves a checkers and whittlers club but mostly what they
do is talk about grass and cattle and make wood shavings
from pieces of lumber. I don't know of anything useful that
was ever whittled.

"You would think they'd get enough of grass and cattle
all week long. But the good thing is that while the women
are shopping or having tea at the hotel dining room we
know where the men are. And in spite of meeting at the
saloon, they do very little drinking.

"Anyways, Dora, you have nothing to worry yourself
about if beauty becomes a talked about thing. You're the
equal to any."

I blushed a bit. "That's very kind, Wanda. Probably not
true but still very kind. I did meet one particularly attractive young woman here. Noah hired her to look after the
place while he was away. Her name is Laura. Very beautiful
and quite bold. I rather thought she and her family might
be here today but I don't see her."

Wanda answered, "She's here. I saw her going into the
bunkhouse. But you won't see her family. They don't mix
much. Stick to themselves mostly."

I nodded and stood up. "If she's in the bunkhouse, I'm
going to see that she feels welcome for the festivities."

Walking through the shade of the yard I was amazed to
see the tables all set up. Someone had found some
sawhorses and covered them with boards and white cloth.
I suspected that some of the cloths were bed sheets.

The plates and bowls were being set out, again being
covered with white cloth to keep the kids and the flies out.
There would be nowhere near enough chairs. But there
was lots of grass to sit on and it was long known that a
cowboy would squat on his heels right beside a good chair,

holding his dinner plate in his hands, and be perfectly content.

I found Laura sitting on a bunk reading a book. At first, she refused to join the group but finally she pulled a brush through her hair, tucked her shirt into her riding skirt and followed me into the yard.

"I appreciate the invite but are you sure it's alright? None of these folks have much truck with my kin. I might make them uncomfortable. They pretty much see us as hillbillies."

It was hard to see how someone so beautiful could have doubts about herself. I wasn't sure how to handle the situation so I simply said, "This is my home and my wedding day and I want you to be here. Don't you be worried about what others think or say."

Laura walked along with me until a young man hollered, "Laura, hello, I didn't know you were here."

Before long she was surrounded by young cowboys, all of them jostling for position around her, so I walked away just in time to hear Mrs. Ransom calling everyone, "Wedding time, folks. Where are the bride and groom? Come on everyone."

I laughed inside, wondering if I'd be like that after thirty or forty years on a ranch. She lacked a little in gentleness but I'd have to admit she got the job done.

We held the wedding on the brick sidewalk just a few feet in front of the veranda steps. The veranda was crowded with watchers while the kids sat on the dried-out grass on either side of the sidewalk. The people who couldn't get on the veranda stood on the grass behind the kids.

I had barely time to rush upstairs and put on my special dress. The way Mrs. Ransom was pushing the event along I was afraid they might start without me.

Noah looked handsome in his new store-bought suit and his white Stetson although when I whispered to him that he might want to take the hat off, he pretended he didn't hear me.

21

NOAH

IT TOOK SO little time to change my life forever that I was still wondering what was going to happen and before I hardly even got my feet planted, it had already happened.

The Reverend Josiah started out alright, making his way from one point to the next quickly. But then he seemed to feel the need to offer advice on marriage, earning his fee so to speak. I don't remember exactly what it was that he said but I'm sure Dora will remind me from time to time.

The next thing I knew, I had said 'I do" to some question that I didn't hear clearly and then I was groping in my vest pocket for the ring we had bought in town. Dora had agreed that we would change the ring after we found a big city jeweler who could make a ring from some of my gold.

Before the ceremony, Josiah had asked who was going to stand up with us. I didn't get his meaning until Dora whispered in my ear. The banker was the only one I knew half well. He agreed to take the position. He and his wife stood beside us while we said the vows. They really had nothing to add but perhaps they made us feel a little less conspicuous standing there in our own front yard with all those strangers looking on.

Josiah suggested that it would be alright if I were to kiss Mrs. Gates. We had kissed once or twice before but we were a long way from what you might call practiced at it so we fumbled a bit but finally the cheering and yelling in the yard signaled that the effort was adequate.

Mercifully, Mrs. Ransom announced in a voice you couldn't ignore that dinner was ready. Dora and I went first past the food table with the others following right along. Soon everyone was seated and quiet.

The afternoon became a steady stream of meeting new folks and hearing new names and listening to idle chatter. But eventually the party started to wind down and again I was shaking hands as people came to say good-bye and wish us happiness. About that time my definition of happiness would have been an empty yard with the rear end of a lot of wagons dusting off in the distance.

I smiled to myself as I watched a family impatiently hollering for a young man who was slowly and reluctantly saying goodbye to Laura. I asked Robb who the young fellow was. He nodded towards him and said, "That's Adam Blossom. Good family. Close neighbors to the H-R. He's a fine young man. Works for me on the H-R from time to time. It's easy to see that he's smitten with Laura. Can't say as how I blame him. She's easy to look at. But I'm kind of afraid that Laura has her eyes on a bigger target." He provided no details.

It pleased Dora that Laura had finally figured out she was no longer employed or required as caretaker of the G-bar. She set out walking for home. I would have lent her a horse had I known soon enough but by the time I noticed, she was already at the end of the quarter-mile-long drive-way. I got the feeling that she didn't much want to go home. I couldn't really blame her thinking back to the rough and ready ranch I had visited weeks before. And then, looking more closely, I saw that Wolf was walking along with Laura. And here I'd let myself believe that Wolf and I had developed an understanding of sorts. Just goes to show that loyalty is harder to come by than most folks think.

Dora excused herself to, as she said, "see what kind of a shambles the house was in." I walked to the barn to check the animals. With those unnecessary chores seen to, we found ourselves sitting in the rocking chairs on the veranda watching the Colorado sky turn from bright blue to a hazier blue, tinged with pink where the setting sun backlit the few clouds that floated over the Front Range. It would be full dark in just no time at all.

The slight chill to the air gave warning that the summer months were past and fall would soon be upon the G-bar.

We were both silent, neither one looking at the other and clearly uneasy about our new situation. Finally, I felt Dora's fingers wrap around my hand as I rested it on the rocker's arm. For some reason, I lifted my Stetson off my head before turning to look at my wife.

She smiled just the smallest of smiles and said, "I do believe I am going to enjoy being Mrs. Noah Gates."

I returned what might have been a grin. "Well, you really had no choice. I told you in the hotel dining room that you couldn't back out after me making a fool of myself in that general store. So here we are. The deed is done and you're my wife. I like the sound of that."

I looked away and then, after a short pause, I said, "If there's any coffee left, would you like some?"

Dora stood up and gave a light pull on my hand. "Neither of us needs any more coffee this night. Come!"

22

NARRATOR

STILL EXPECTING a posse to be chasing them, the Barger gang headed south and a bit west back to where they had left their stolen horse herd with three riders to guard them. Barger figured they had better lay low for a while. The first night out, they camped along a bend of the Arkansas River, taking their cold supper below the cut bank. Lighting a fire was out of the question on these mostly treeless prairies if they didn't want to give away their location. They were in the saddle well before first light the next morning hoping to get to the Cherokee lands that same day. After a long hard ride, Barger led his exhausted gang under the lip of a rock and clay overhang and into a cluster of bush along the Cimarron River. There they joined the men and horses they had left behind and camped for a week, feeling it was safe enough to rest up for a spell. The men rested and cared for their horses. A few of them washed their clothes in the river and, although there

was a fall chill in the air, most of them took the opportunity to bathe off the accumulation of sweat and road dust.

Barger spent the week deep in thought. He called the
men together after breakfast. "Men, we got to make some
changes. This country is settling up and the law is getting
more organized. It was bad enough with the telegraph
covering nearly the whole of the country. Now the bigger
towns are starting to get this new telephone machine. We
can't outrun either of those. And there's getting to be just
too many people.

"We have to find a new country to work from. I'm too
old to change my ways and probably wouldn't even if I had
the chance. I doubt as how any of you want to go back to
the farm either. We're going further west. A lot further. I've
been hearing about the new mining towns out past the
western mountains. Been hearing about their need for
riding and work animals. Been hearing about the color
that's being pulled from the mines, too. I figure that
country holds more promise than where we been up
to now.

"We'll break camp this morning. Ride out two by two.
Drive a few loose horses each. We'll find a market for them
out west. Take whatever route you want, stay out of trouble, talk to no one, and we'll come together again in three
weeks. I ain't never been west and don't know the country.
Any of you ever been there?"

"I have," answered a rider named Kowalski.

Barger nodded at him. "We need a place to meet. Do
you have a place comes to mind?"

Kowalski thought for a moment. "There's a little saloon
just on the south side of Denver by a few miles. Names
'Ace's'. Ace don't ask questions or offer answers. Good
place to wait around till we all get there."

Barger nodded at him again. "Then that's what we'll do.

Take your time and don't do anything to bring attention on yourselves. I may be a couple of days late but I'll get there by-and-by. I have to ride north a ways and visit a man called Trembley. Got a bit of business with him. Then I'll come right along."

Within an hour, the campground was empty and the gang was heading west in five small groups; four groups of three men and Barger riding alone on the big red stallion he had taken in a raid further east in Indian Territory the year before. The gang of twelve had been reduced to nine with the shooting in Kansas plus the three riders that had stayed with the horse herd.

Most of the men arrived at Ace's Saloon before the three weeks were up. They took it easy, sleeping late and keeping out of trouble. Mason Benson took the leadership while they waited for Barger who was several days late. When he finally rode into town and entered the saloon, Benson quietly asked, "Everything go alright, boss?" Barger just nodded and raised his glass.

After a short time of visiting and talking about the trails and the country around, Barger spoke to Kowalski, "You've been here before. You ever seen a map of this area?"

"Never did before," answered Kowalski, "but I found one just yesterday down at the newspaper printers." He laid it out on the saloon table.

The map was a crudely-drawn approximation of the area around Denver and the mountains to the north and west. It mostly faded out before the Wyoming border but it included a few details around Fort Collins. Barger held the map in his hands for a short while. "Anyone know exactly what's up here?"

He was pointing at a pencil line that showed a trail running from the Colorado side of the mountains all the way into Utah. He had to squint and hold the paper up to the light coming through the window to see the faintly-penciled name clearly. "Poudre River," he said, having trouble with the pronunciation. Looking up at the men, he tapped the paper with his finger. "This here Poudre River seems to have a valley that goes right the way through the mountains. At least it's drawn that way on this paper. We would have to ride north a ways and then swing west up into the hills. We'll leave first light tomorrow morning."

Benson gave his boss a questioning look. "That's just a hand-drawn map, boss. No telling who drew it or if they knew what was right and what was wrong. There's been lots of surveying done out here, mostly by the military. Might be we could get better information if we look around some."

Barger, never one to tolerate someone second-guessing him, gave Benson a withering look. "We leave at first light."

"All I'm saying, boss, is that we're staking a lot on a pencil line on a piece of paper."

Barger got up and left the room, not saying where he was going. No one asked or followed.

Into the silence that overshadowed the room with Barger's leaving, Kowalski said, "That's it, I guess, for better or worse. Don't know what any of you plan for the afternoon but I need to buy some cold-weather gear and get my horse shod. Need some trail supplies, too. See y'all later." He followed Barger out the door.

None of the other men spoke but one by one they drained their glasses and left to attend to their own plans and needs.

Daylight found the gang on the trail north, taking a wide turn around Denver and lining out for Fort Collins and the Poudre River. They swung to the east taking advantage of flatter land. They saw Fort Collins off to the west but kept going north to avoid drawing attention to themselves. Although the military had been gone for some years, the Fort Collins name had remained and a thriving settlement had grown up around the old post.

They ended up further north than they had planned. Two days later, they swung west into the foothills and the edge of the hilly ranching country.

Barger didn't know the country to the west and neither did any of his men. He had put considerable trust in saloon talk and campfire visits back in Indian Territory and the talk picked up from the old timers he had found around Ace's Saloon. Barger was an Easterner, basically a flat-lander, except for his youth in Missouri which he had mostly tried to forget about.

What he didn't understand was that when a mountain man talked about a river or a creek or a turn in the trail, he was talking about a very specific location and if you missed that location or the bend in the river mentioned, you could end up in a totally different situation than the one planned. He also didn't understand that few travelers had reason to follow a river valley any further than necessary. So what might be true of the Poudre River near Fort Collins would not necessarily be true further into the mountains.

On the flat grassland where there were no mountains or river gorges dividing up the land, there was room to make a correction in the travel. It was not like that in the Western country. Unaware of the hazards of the river and feeling the pressure of winter coming on, Barger was becoming careless, pushing his men and horses towards a valley that existed mostly in his imagination.

"Men, somewhere up there is what they call the 'Great Divide'. That's said to be the highest point of land along this area. The rivers flow to the west on one side and to the east on the other. All we have to do is connect with one of them there west-flowing rivers and we'll be in Utah before you know it."

He could see that the land ahead was nothing like he had been told or had imagined but he kept his doubts to himself. When he had heard the stories of the western mountains in the saloons back east, he imagined the hills of his Missouri home. But days before as he had approached Bent's Old Fort and started riding further north and west towards Ace's Saloon, he got his first real look at the Rockies in all their snowcapped grandeur. With that first glance at the glacier-topped mountains beyond the foothills, he had pulled his horse to a stop, staring in awe. What stood ahead of him was unimaginable. The Rockies were like something he had never seen or pictured before and he knew he was in trouble.

Still, he had never been a quitter and his men weren't the kind who would follow a weak leader. And there was nothing to go back east to so he was pushing the men and animals onward towards what he hoped was a gateway to Utah and the lands beyond.

Eastern Colorado was mostly open, unfenced, short-grass country which the men had moved through easily. But towards the foothills where water was more plentiful, there were farms and smaller ranches, many of them fenced and all of them hilly with a fair scattering of brush and forest preventing him from seeing what was ahead.

Their going was slowed by the desire to by-pass the small ranches and farms. They tried traveling at night but kept running into barbwire fencing that couldn't be seen until it was too late to avoid the trap. They had one good thing in their favor; there was grass and water everywhere with no need to search it out.

The gang wound its tedious way through a rock- and

forest-covered series of hills as they neared the foothills of the Front Range. Now, riding up a sizable hillside, Barger put a scout named Bentley out front to sort out a path westward. They had been riding among a scattering of cattle for most of the day and that worried Barger, not wishing to run into a cowboy or anyone else who might ask him to explain himself.

Just as they were nearing the crest of the highest hill that would lead to the downward slope and open the way west, Bentley returned. "Boss, there's at least three ranches in that valley ahead. Can't see their buildings but they all have windmills showing and wood smoke rising from cooking fires. Everything that way is fenced. There might be a way through those rough hills if we were to circle around to the south but I didn't have time to check it out. Or we could drive down the road and bluff our way through if someone was to question us. We did that before and had no trouble."

Barger nodded at this report and stood in his stirrups, looking all around. Finally, he turned to his scout. "Bentley, take Jamison with you and scout those hills to the south. We'll hold here until you get back. I don't want to run into a problem so we'll try to avoid those ranches."

Bentley and Jamison were back within a couple of hours with a report. "It ain't easy but there's a way through. This bush skirts a couple of ranches and then opens up to the west. We could get through but anyone seeing us would wonder why we're there. It still might be better to take the road. We could pass for cowboys looking for work."

Barger ignored their concerns and said, "Lead out. Let's get through here as fast as we can."

The trail they chose followed along the Circle-S fence line that enclosed the mountain grassland that had been turned over to summer grazing for the Stanton ranch remuda. Barger stopped to look over the fenced-in horses. He pulled off to one side to allow his own small herd to go past and then called over three of his riders. "Butler, cut down a couple of sections of that fence. Those are fine-looking horses and I want them. But we'll have to be quick about it."

The fence was soon down and the three thieves rode a wide circle around the remuda before pushing them towards the fence line. A few horses balked at the approaching wire but when one old mare with a colt at foot walked between the posts, the rest finally followed.

"Push them easy until they settle down," Barger hollered.

Within one-half hour, the two groups of horses were driven together and they proceeded south and a little west still following the fence.

Just as they were approaching the end of the brush and hill country with forest and mountains ahead, they came upon another small gathering of summered-out horses. Within a short while, these too - all carrying the C/R brand - were added to the herd of stolen animals. Barger looked at the horses gathered ahead of him with a satisfied smirk. He saw only profit; he had no real love or appreciation for horses. He would drive them as hard as necessary to get them through to Utah and on to Nevada. If they lost a few along the way, he would shrug it off as a cost of doing business.

They passed a ranch house in the distance and veered further into the trees. Barger spoke to the two men riding beside him, "Schultz, you and Ike keep these nags moving along. I'm riding forward to set the trail. Keep them closed up and don't let them wander off."

Schultz watched as Barger rode around the herd. He

looked over at his riding partner. "Ike, I'm thinking our leader has gone a bit over the edge. He's likely to get us all jailed or hung. Cutting fences and grabbing horses in a settled area is a bit too much for me. And if that's not enough, take a look at those mountains ahead. If there's a way through that pile of rock and ice for all these horses, I'll be surprised. I see nothing up there but trouble and grief. The more I think about it, the more I miss Missouri. And the way I figure it, the quicker I head that way the quicker I'll be back there. I wouldn't mind having a riding partner on the way back. What do you say?"

Ike pulled his horse to a stop and spat a wad of chaw off to the side. "We'd have to leave with nothing. Our bedrolls and such are on the packhorses up front. And I was planning on a cut from the selling of this here herd. Still, I've got a few dollars in my pocket and I've ridden the grub line before. Going to jail is no part of my thinking and being hung just holds no attraction at all."

Schultz nodded his head towards where the packhorses were bunched up. "Ain't much of a herd left to sell even with these we just picked up. After we split it twelve ways, we'd be better off stealing penny candy from kids. Anyway, I ain't never been no thief and the thought makes me uncomfortable. You and I, we've closed our eyes to some things these past weeks because other work is nigh on impossible to find but I doubt as how we can keep doing that. I think it's time we cut our losses."

Schultz pointed a careless hand towards where the pack animals were being herded. "And everything I own that's packed onto that nag up ahead ain't worth a ten-dollar gold piece. I have enough coin in my jeans to buy a few meals along the way and a new blanket, one without holes in it. And right about now I'd gladly ride the night herd on some ranch if it meant sleeping in a bunk and eating three squares a day. I'm getting mighty tired of the trail. We ain't seen a dollar of profit for two months and Utah and Nevada are still a long ways off."

Ike nodded and spat again. Schultz took that as agreement and turned his horse around, kicking it into an easy trot. Ike soon caught up to him. "Let's head a bit to the east and north. Get away from that trail we left through the bush and away from these ranches."

The two men were soon over a small hill and out of sight. The trailing horses were left to do as they pleased.

Within an hour, the men riding the flanks of the herd rode back to see why the animals were so spread out. It soon became obvious what had happened. They swung in behind the trailing horses and began closing up the remnants of the herd. A few had surely wandered off but they didn't have time to go after them.

The group of thieves was now down to ten men. Barger flew into a rage at this latest bit of news but he knew it would be pointless to try to catch the deserters. With gritted teeth, he drove men and horses relentlessly towards the waiting hills.

They left the last ranch behind them, skirted a small Indian reserve, and moved southwest. Arriving at the banks of a river they took to be the Poudre, they swung west following the river valley into the mountains. Before long they were surrounded by forest-covered hills. But the river they were following had wide banks so the going looked to be easy. They gathered the horses into a rope corral and went into camp for the night.

NOAH

THE FIRST TWO weeks of marriage seemed to sweep past so quickly it was hard to get my mind around it all. Dora was clearly more in control of herself than I was. She hummed a tuneless melody as she strolled through the house, examining every tiniest bit of it for perhaps the tenth time. She picked up the few ornaments and trinkets that had been left from the previous owners, examining them and setting them down. She took a careful study of the Indian artifacts and old guns on the mantle and on the shelves in the ranch house office. Once, turning to leave the little office, she bumped right into me standing there with my hat on and my hands in my pockets. She gave a startled yelp and then started to laugh. She shook her head and made her way past me and out the door.

Putting a meal together in her own kitchen had her singing right out loud while I found myself standing on one foot and then the other, uncomfortable with all the newness and with nothing at all to do. I had tried to tell Dora that I wasn't totally housebroken and I think she was coming to believe it.

The only relief I found was tending to the imaginary chores I created in the barn or when I was tending to the small herd of horses running loose in the pasture. Even caring for the horses was an imagined task. They were fine without me and could have been left to themselves for the rest of the fall and the winter, too, for that matter. I would be adding a herd of breeding animals in the spring but that still left a long winter ahead of me.

As I studied on the few horses on the G-bar, my mind wandered to the big red stallion I had lost. He had been my riding horse. Most stallions make for poor riding but Red had been a wonder of strength and gentleness. Lying on my lonely tack room bunk back in that livery barn I owned, I had imagined pastures alive with the colts from the red stallion. I missed him more than any of the other stolen animals.

I split and hauled so much firewood into the kitchen that Dora started to laugh when I showed up with my arms full again. "You're bored. I can see that it's going to be a long winter with you pacing the floor and looking out one window and then another. You'll be talking out loud to yourself if you don't find something to do. I'm sure all the barn chores are done and you just had break- fast and you've drunk more coffee than any one man needs. You've got the whole day ahead of you. Why don't you saddle up and ride to town? I'm baking bread so I have to stay here but I think an afternoon in town would do you good. I have a short list of things I need from the store and who can tell, you might run into someone you know or maybe even meet someone new. I'm sure there's new gossip to pick up, too. We can never have too much gossip." She had a bit of a grin on her face as she said this.

She ended this lengthy speech by patting my unshaven cheek and presenting me with a lingering kiss that almost convinced me to stay home. But the draw of a few miles of riding and an hour in town was strong. So after assuring myself that she would be alright alone, I saddled up. She waved from the porch and I tipped my hat as I rode out.

In town, my first stop was at Green's Mercantile. After stowing the few store purchases in my saddlebag, I walked over to the blacksmith shop. A few simple words of greeting led me to placing a small order. "I need a G-bar branding iron. Something not more than two inches high and made from light metal. I sketched it in the dust of his single windowsill while he looked on.

At the blacksmith's quizzical look, I explained, "I'm going to be breeding horses for sale. I found I get a better price if their hides are unmarked so I just give them a small brand up high on the neck where the mane will cover it. Just enough to prove my ownership if anyone should make a challenge. I need you to put together something small that will do that job."

The blacksmith, a man of few words and of even fewer smiles, nodded his understanding. "Give me a few days." He turned back to his forge showing no interest in further talk so I started back across the street to my horse.

The hitch rail in front of the general store which had been empty when I rode in an hour earlier now had two new horses tied beside my bay. I ignored a black I had never seen before but I immediately recognized the second animal; a gray gelding with a blond, almost white mane and two white stocking on his front feet. An easy horse to recognize and remember.

Well, seeing that horse set me up some and stopped me

dead in my tracks. After a long study of the horse, I edged closer, scanning the street for his rider. By instinct my hand fell to the handle of my Colt, lifting it slightly to loosen it in the holster. As the years passed, there were fewer and fewer men carrying sidearms but I still felt naked without mine. Perhaps the time would come for me to hang it on a hook at home but that time was not yet. I walked around the horse to get a look at his brand. On his left hip was burned a Lazy–S that was new since I had last seen the animal. Stepping towards the horse's head, I gave his neck a gentle rub and spoke softly to him. Still rubbing his neck, I slid my other hand up under his mane, running my fingers along until I felt something. I pushed the hair aside and there in small letters, hidden under that silver-white mane, was my G-bar.

After all the months of riding and looking, I had pretty much given up any thought of finding any of my stolen animals and now this gray was all but offered up to me on a platter. I lifted my hat and ran my fingers through my hair while looking around again for the rider. Finally deciding the riders must be in the general store, I stepped up onto the walkway and moved towards the door.

The little brass bell tinkled when I pushed the door open. At the noise, Adam Green, the storekeeper, glanced up and the two men at the counter both turned and glanced over their shoulders to see who had stepped inside. What they saw was me with my hand on my Colt and a no-nonsense look on my face. Nothing in my life had led me towards carelessness so I was ready for whatever might happen next.

"If you get smart and don't move, you men just might live to grow another day older." All three froze in place.

"Green, you step aside. You other two, very slowly press your hands onto the countertop and keep your eyes on the back bar. If you reach for a weapon, you will die right where you stand. You might think you have a chance to draw and turn but you have just no chance at all. You do as I say now and we'll all be still breathing an hour from now."

They did as I said but one of them, a big man with a rain-ruined hat and ragged range clothes and worn-out boots with run-over heels, growled at me with a deep bass voice, "You got no cause to call us out, mister. We been here less than a half-hour and all we want is some trail provisions and we'll be on our way. We mean no harm."

I stepped towards them and gently lifted their sidearms. "I'll decide on all of that."

Stepping back, I said, "Alright, turn around now and tell me which of you is riding that gray gelding out there and then tell me where you got him."

The smaller and equally-ragged of the two nodded towards the window and the hitch rail outside. "That's my horse. Got him down in the Nations a while ago. What's it to you what horse a man rides. It's a free country; man can ride whatever horse he wants and not answer to every country bumpkin that comes along."

I looked over at Green. "Green, I'd appreciate if you could holler up the sheriff. Tell him there's a horse thief in your store just waiting for him to come with those wrist irons he carries with him."

I looked back at the men. "As for you naming me as a country bumpkin, you need to know that the only reason you're still standing upright is because I've turned over a new leaf so to speak. I just got married a short while back and I made myself a promise that I wouldn't shoot anyone else for at least a month or two. Of course, no one knows about that promise except me so if I were to break it, I could get over the disappointment in myself pretty quick, although I do hate to break a promise." The whole speech was a shameful exaggeration but it seemed to have the desired effect.

The two men watched Green walking towards the door and seemed to flinch in unison when the little brass bell tinkled.

I spoke again to the men, "That G-bar gray is mine. He was stolen down in the Nations last year along with my entire herd of trade horses. Unless you can show me a legitimate bill of sale, I'm looking at a horse thief."

The rider pointed with his jaw at the horses outside. "I never heard of no G-bar. The horse carried that 'Lazy-S' when I got him, no other brand. And I've got a bill of sale stashed in a saddlebag. It's a bit crumpled and weathered but it's still readable. You're wrong, mister, and given a fair shake I'd take you down a notch or two." He glanced up again as the brass bell tinkled and Green walked in with a man wearing a silver star.

Sheriff Howard looked at me. "What's this about horses, Gates?"

"Welcome to our little party, Sheriff. I'm going to ask you to step out and lift the mane on that gray and then come back in and tell us what you found."

The sheriff stared at me for a moment and then stepped outside. Again, the tinkle of the bell caused the men to flinch as if that bell was tolling out their life's minutes and was more dangerous to them than my Colt or the sheriff, either one.

We all stood in silence and waited. In less than a minute, the bell tinkled again and the sheriff came in leaving the door open behind him. A rather buxom lady all full of hurry and self-importance, her petticoats fluffing her long dress out in all directions, followed him in. Green glanced over at her. "Mable, we have a situation here. It would be better if you were to come back later."

Clearly Mable was all set to argue her rights but without turning around, the sheriff said firmly, "Close the door on your way out, Mable." Mable pursed her lips as if to say more but the sheriff gave her no opportunity. "Now, Mable." With a huff, she was gone. I wouldn't have thought it of the easygoing sheriff but his 'Now' was like a command or at least Mable took it as such.

The sheriff saw the empty holsters on the men's hips and nodded his partial satisfaction. "If either of you two are carrying a holdout weapon, it would be best if you told me now. Might save you getting dead."

Hearing nothing from either man, Howard said, "Step close together and stretch out your right hands." When the men raised their hands, he clamped the wrist irons on them. "Just have the one set with me so that will have to do." The two handcuffed men stood there awkwardly with the smaller one's right arm stretched across his body to meet the arm of his partner.

Sheriff Wilson grinned over at me. "Hard for these boys to run trussed up like that. If they should take a notion to is what I mean. Watched a couple of boys try it one time. Put on a real show for the townsfolk, tripping and falling all over themselves, their arms all in a tangle.

"Now you men, we have a peaceable town here. Don't much care for any ruction. You just need to see how quietly you can walk over to that jailhouse across the road."

The larger of the two started walking but his smaller partner tugged him to a stop. "This is a mistake, Sheriff. That's my horse, fair and square. That's no G-bar animal as this bozo claims. I ain't never heard of the G-bar."

The sheriff pushed him forward towards the door.

"Going to be pretty difficult to explain that G-bar brand under all that pretty white hair then. Walk. You can tell your story over at the jail or wait until the judge gets to town if he ever does. It's up to you but you need to understand; I'm not a real patient sort. Kind of like to wrap things up neat and quick, if you know what I mean. Might go easier on you were you to fess up the truth before this all goes any further."

I followed the sheriff onto the sidewalk. He nudged the prisoners down onto the dusty road and started across to the jail. Mable stood just outside the store door, huffed up like a barn-fed pigeon. As soon as we cleared the doorway, she strutted back into the store, a determined swagger to her steps. I didn't envy Green as I heard him say, "What can I do for you, Mable?"

As the sheriff prodded the two men across the road, I untied my horse and led him and the other two to the shade of the livery stable. Then I walked back to the jailhouse.

Once the two riders were searched for holdout weapons and stowed safely behind bars, Sheriff Howard took a seat behind his clean-topped desk. As I watched him search the men, I came up with a new respect for our small-town sheriff. He saw me looking at his actions and showed a slight grin. "Got careless once. Didn't bother to search a pleasant-looking young cowboy who had been causing a bit of a turmoil over in a tent saloon brought on by too much snake juice. That was over in Arizona. The firewater they served as drinking material in that filthy tent establishment had been the cause of more than one problem. But judging by his pleasant looks alone, I put that cowboy into a cell and turned my back, thinking he would lie down and pass out while he sobered up. But no such a thing happened.

"What he did was, he pulls out a boot gun and shoots

the lock off the cell door and then drew a bead on me. I dove behind my desk and we had a hot time of it for the next few seconds, exchanging shots until we both ran out of ammunition. The thing is, though, I had a second gun in a desk drawer and he was empty of bullets. Only one possible outcome given that situation." Howard chuckled and shook his head remembering the incident.

One of the prisoners was listening to this story and I wasn't sure if the tale was true or just something Howard made up to scare the boys in the cell. Anyway, the big one spoke up, "What happened to the cowboy?"

Howard chuckled again and shook his head as if he was telling a story at a family gathering. "Oh, him. Well, after the doc dug the lead out and fixed up his bullet-smashed leg, that old boy hobbled his way into the circuit court and was sent to Yuma. Kind of a shame what a bother can come out of a bottle of red-eye. Nice young kid, too. But I surely don't take to getting shot at. I expect he'll get out some day but not for a while. Trying to shoot an officer of the law isn't taken lightly in Arizona or anywhere else I know of.

"I wouldn't want that to happen to you boys. It's bad enough to get hung for horse-stealing but to get sent to Yuma, too, is not something to look forward to. Of course, it might depend on whether Yuma comes first or the hanging. I'd have to admit there is a sight of difference between the two options."

Sheriff Howard pulled a hardback notebook from a desk drawer, licked the end of a pencil and looked back over at his prisoners. "Now, boys, let's talk. Just friendly like, you know, like we were old riding pards or some such, sitting around waiting for the beans to finish cooking. Only difference is that I usually knew the names of my riding pards so let's start there."

He pointed his pencil at the big one. "Let's start with

you. What did your Momma call you and what name do you go by on the trail?"

The rider was all set to be stubborn but finally decided against it. "They call me 'Schultz'. He made no motion towards giving any additional information."

"Well, that's a start anyway. We'll stick with that until I get time to look over that stack of wanted posters." Howard tapped his pencil and looked at the smaller of the two; saying nothing, just waiting.

After a long pause, the rider came out with a single word, "Ike."

Howard smiled the way a coyote might smile if he were to find the chicken coop door left open.

"OK, Schultz and Ike, what's your story? You said you were just passing along this way and were heading out as soon as you purchased some trail fixings. But the thing is, there's just no reason for anyone to be passing along this way. Our little town is north of Denver and south of Cheyenne and a far ways west of the traveled road. A body would have to be either lost or up to some mischief to arrive here in Canyon View. It ain't likely you was just happening by. So, let's start over with the real story.

"We already know one of you is riding a stolen horse. Can't really tell about the other one without I send wires all around the country asking about the brand. Or I could take a ride into Fort Collins and find me one of them there telephones I keep hearing about. Gates here says the second animal isn't his but if you stole one, I would have to believe you might have stolen them both."

After a short pause while he continued tapping his pencil on the book, Howard looked back up at the men. "You promise not to repeat it, boys, and I'll tell you a secret. You see, I like this little town. Good folks and not too much to disturb a man's life. Wife plays the organ over at that little church. All in all, we've got it pretty good. Hate to see any of that change.

"As I told you before, we don't care for a lot of ruction. And I admit to being just a little bit lazy. It would suit my laziness if I were to find a reason to open that door and watch you fellers ride away. It would save me a sight of paperwork and all the bother of feeding you which I admit to having forgot to do in times past.

"So, tell me about the horse and what you're really doing in our fair town."

The pause was long and the silence felt like midnight on the range with the cattle settled down and the snoring cowboys far enough away to be out of hearing.

Howard had that pasted-on grin aimed at the prisoners and he stared unblinking for so long that I started wondering how long he could hold the gaze. I had never seen anyone go that long without blinking. It started to become unnerving to me. And I was on the right side of the cell bars.

Ike and Schultz watched the sheriff for a few moments and then took a long study of each other. I couldn't read their thoughts but somehow I got the feeling that Howard knew exactly what they were thinking and what they were going to do next. Again, my respect for the sheriff grew.

Ike broke off his gaze, turning and walking to the other side of the small cell. He flopped down onto the hard bunk for a moment and I saw his lips moving as if he was talking to himself, figuring things out. His lips stopped moving and he slowly got to his feet. When he stepped to the cell bars, it was clear he had made a decision. Schultz aimed a worried look at him. "Ike, don't you do anything foolish."

Ike spoke to Schultz without looking at him, "What's foolish is us standing here helpless behind these bars with that fat excuse for a lawman sitting out there grinning at us and us innocent of the horse-stealing we're being accused of."

If he somehow thought that calling me a country bumpkin or Howard a fat excuse for a sheriff was going to be helpful to his cause he was sadly mistaken.

Ike put his arms through the bars and leaned on the flat iron piece that ran across the bars halfway between the floor and the low ceiling. "I'll talk to you, Sheriff. But first you got to tell me what you want to hear that will open this door for Schultz and me. I ain't going to tell you my entire life story." He looked first at me and then at Howard and then back at me.

Howard broke off his staring and grinning long enough to look over at me. "The gray is your G-bar animal, Gates. Tell the man what you want."

"That's simple for me, Sheriff. I just want my horse back and the story about how this man comes to be riding him, and if he has any idea what became of the rest of my herd. As to the bill of sale he showed us, it tells us nothing at all I can hang my hat on."

Howard pasted the grin back on and somehow talked through it, "There you go, Ike."

Ike wasn't entirely happy with the answer. "That's as well as might be, Sheriff. But it's you that holds the key to this door not the country bumpkin."

The grin disappeared and a serious look took its place. "Here's the way of it, son, as I see it right now. That horse was clearly stolen, whether by you or by the man you say you bought it from. I don't know the truth of that and have no way of sorting it all out. I could simply take your word for it but then I'm willing to speculate that you haven't told the truth since you got caught stealing an apple pie off the neighbor's window sill.

"Of course, I might learn more were I to send those

wires I talked about to all the lawmen east of here. Or pull out all those wanted posters off those shelves over there and look through them. But then that's a lot of work and I already told you I'm just a little bit lazy so I'd rather not have to do all of that.

"No, what Gates wants is his horse back and what I want is the truth about why we have the pleasure of your company in our little town. I suspect there's a bigger story here than that one stolen horse. You give me that story and make me believe it and I'll see if I can't find the key to that door."

Again, Ike paced the floor before putting his arms back through the cell bars. Schultz whispered to him but I had no trouble hearing the words, "Barger will hunt us down and kill us." It was a warning spoken from fear.

Ike looked at his riding partner. He didn't seem to care that we could hear. "Barger's going to have a lot more trouble than what you and I can provide. I'm guessing he'll be dead within the week and us with him if we hadn't pulled out."

Ike pinned the sheriff with a steady gaze. "I've spent no time at all teaching Sunday school, Sheriff. But on the other hand, I've never done anything to get my name on one of those posters you keep talking about. I'm just a forty a month and found rider put out of work by the stringing of bob wire. A lot of good men are riding the grub line these days, honest men who had their way of life taken from them. Ranchers don't hire hardly any riders anymore and I don't have much else I can do. Things get any worse I'll be shoveling in a livery barn and sleeping in the tack room just to earn grub.

"Schultz and I met a few months ago, both of us down on our luck and me without a horse. I owned a good ride but had to shoot the poor beast when he swole all up on his front leg after being snake bit.

"We were spending some of the last of our funds on a plate of stew and biscuits in this little greasy spoon shack in a nowhere town when a feller down the table spoke, "'Could use a couple more riders if you two are so inclined.'"

"Well, I looked around behind me thinking maybe he was speaking to someone else. But then he said it again directly at me and nodding at Schultz. About that time, I figured that something was better than nothing. When one thing finished leading to another, we hired on and he sold me that gray along with a bill of sale for fifty dollars payment to be made from the first of my earned wages.

"We didn't know what the crew was up to, sitting out for several weeks and herding a collection of horses along a river valley over in the Nations. But the grub was good so we stuck it out. Then, a few weeks ago, we ups and starts west driving those horses, just following orders to earn our keep. A few days ago, it all started to come clear; Schultz and me, we waited our chance and lit a shuck. That's the whole of it."

Howard was looking at the two prisoners and tapping the pencil against his teeth. After a minute of this, he looked over at me. "What do you think, Gates? You happy with your part of it? You lead that pretty little gray home and find contentment on your G-bar with your horses and your new wife."

I answered, "That's a good part of it, Sheriff, but I want to know who Ike got the horse from and if there were any other G-bar animals in their herd."

Ike had gone that far and he wasn't holding anything back anymore. "Got the animal from a feller named Barger. Phil Barger. He was the leader of the crew and the one who hired us. Signed a bill of sale for me. As to other G-bar animals, I wouldn't know. With that mane brand you were using, we wouldn't have seen the G-bar if it was there. Most of the animals were Lazy-S with a scattering of other burns."

I acknowledged the right of what he said about the mane brand but then, "I didn't always use the mane brand. Only thought of it after a buyer commented that he wished the hide on the horse he was purchasing was slick. Lots of animals around with left hip G-bar brands."

I nodded at Howard and he turned to Ike. "Alright, Ike, Gates will settle for that much. Now, you tell me about this Barger; where he is now and what he's doing."

Schultz warned Ike again but Ike ignored him. "We were hired on to drive a herd of trade animals into Utah and Nevada. A hard three-week drive got us into the hills south and west of here. The sight of those mountains scared the boys but Barger promised there was a trail through. Schultz and I were finding some serious doubts.

"And then a couple of days ago Barger up and has some boys cut a fence and drive out a dozen Circle S animals. We didn't like that none at all but as a part of the crew we were trapped. A few hours later he did the same with a bunch of C/R animals. That was more than Schultz and I were willing to be involved with.

"Barger put us bringing up the drag while he went ahead to find a trail. When we got back to the drag position, we just kept a-going in the other direction. I never abandoned a job of work before but I've never been a thief either. We left out of there with all our gear and our earned wages lost to us. That's all there is."

Howard practically laughed right out loud. "Alright, boys. I'm going to turn you loose, taking a chance on your story. You can ride double, walk, or buy a ten-dollar horse at the livery. But I want you out of town within the hour and I never want to see you again.

"I don't know who this Barger is but I sure know the Circle S and the C/R. The Circle S is a fighting outfit that moved in here from Texas a few years ago and the C/R is Clark Ransom's outfit. Barger couldn't have chosen two tougher brands to cast a rope on. Those two old fools that own the Circle S and the C/R would rather fight than eat. And fight each other if no other option presents itself. This Barger ain't never seen the like.

"Only thing the thieves could have done that might be worse was to tie onto some nags from that Kentucky transplant. Him and his brood of tall gangly sons. Abner's his name. That man is never without his long gun and seems disappointed when he has no one to shoot. Worst thing Barger could possibly do would be to grab an Abner animal. Of course, Abner will join in a gathering up of horse thieves even if none of his own animals are involved. Yes, I'd say this Barger will have his hands full."

24

NOAH

I STEPPED across the street and purchased a halter and rope from Green, then led the gray over to the small sheriff's office, dropping Ike's saddle and bridle onto the wooden sidewalk. Howard said he would turn Schultz and Ike loose just as soon as I was out of town. He wanted to get a bit more information out of them hoping to find out where the gang was most likely to be. I told him I would head out over east to warn the Circle S in case they hadn't missed their remuda yet.

I covered the eight miles to the H-R at a ground-eating trot and swung onto their ranch trail under a big, log entryway. An attractive young woman I remembered meeting at the wedding heard the dog bark and stepped onto the ranch house porch. She gave me a careful study before recognition came. "Mr. Gates, how nice of you to visit. What brings you over this way?"

I tipped my hat just a bit. "Afternoon, ma'am. I was

heading to the Circle S when I saw your gate and remembered that you're a Circle S Stanton. I need to get a piece of
news to your dad. Do I keep on east to get there? I haven't
been out this way before."

"Just four miles further east, Mr. Gates, but now you
have me curious. What news are you speaking of? Not
something troublesome I hope."

I lifted my hat and ran my fingers through my hair
while I wondered how much I should say. Some women
don't take to bad news but I could have known that this
ranch wife, like my own Dora, would stand up and face
trouble right along with their men.

"If the news impacts on my family, Mr. Gates, you had
just as well out with it. I'm not at all happy with secrets."

I couldn't hide a grin.

"How does bad news and a grin go together, Mr.
Gates?" Her question showed the beginnings of
impatience.

"I certainly mean no disrespect, Mrs. Robb. I'm just
thinking how it is that ranch women stand by their men
and their families. In those penny magazines the townsfolk
love to read back east, the women are always lost or
fainting or needing to be rescued. But I ain't never met a
western woman like that yet.

"The trouble is about horses. The sheriff put the scare
into a couple of riders passing through town. One of them
was riding this gray. The animal was stolen from me last
year. Funny he should show up in Canyon View. Howard
pressured those boys into telling their story and it turns
out the bunch they'd been riding with cut a Circle S fence a
couple of days ago and helped themselves to some of your
father's horses. Done the same over at the C/R. I thought
I'd ride on over and let them know in case they haven't
been out to the pasture."

Wanda Robb looked startled. "Mr. Gates, when my father and my two brothers find out their horses were stolen there's likely to be an explosion like you've never seen. And the C/R is a whole other issue. Old Clark Ransom isn't happy unless he's fighting or spitting and to have someone foolish enough to – well, I just can't imagine."

I turned my horse, ready to take my leave but then thought about this woman's husband, Hamilton I remembered his name was. "Is your husband somewhere that I can ride by and advise him? Perhaps he should check your stock as well."

"No need to find him, Mr. Gates. I'll just call him. He'll show up soon enough."

With that she strode over to the heavy post firmly embedded in the ground just at the edge of the ranch yard. On the post hung the biggest iron bell I had ever seen. The bell must have been without a clapper because Mrs. Robb picked up a short-handled blacksmith's hammer that hung off a short chain and gave the bell three hard whacks. I thought the clanging bell could probably be heard in town and my horses certainly heard it. They set to jumping and twisting until I finally got them settled down.

I rode over to the bell and looked at it. "Thunderation, Mrs. Robb, wherever in the world did you find that thing? Sounds to me like it might raise the dead like on judgment day or something."

She smiled up at me. "I don't know about raising the dead but it always raises my husband. I expect he was taking a nap under a shade tree over there." She pointed down the slope and across a half-mile pasture to the hills and forest beyond; a nice herd of fat Herefords scattered over the grass. A rider was just coming out of the trees and heading towards the yard.

I took a look around the ranch yard and down the slope at the pasture, hay meadows, stacked hay, water tank and such. "Don't appear to be much napping done around here, judging by looks. Been a sight of work done here to put all this together."

"I'm joking, Mr. Gates. I don't believe Hamilton would even know what a nap was although he's been known to sit out a winter afternoon reading by the fire.

"He'll be here in a short while and I'll get him to check the stock. I'd be obliged if you could go tell the Circle S. Leave the gray here with me; I'll put him in the corral and you can pick him up on your way back. Hamilton will show you the bush trail to your place. It's really only a short ride from here when you know where the trails are."

I rode into the Circle S a half-hour later. A man just coming out of the barn hailed me and I rode over. "Howdy, Noah, just out seeing the country?"

"We'll it's a good country to see but there's more purpose than that. I know we met at the wedding but I didn't get but a few of the names. Sorry about that."

"I'm Sam. My brother is Benjamin and my father is Bob. Some call him Big Bob although that was more down in Texas than it is here. Got a sister, Wanda, married the neighbor and lives just west of here."

"I just came from the H-R. Talked with Mrs. Robb and told her why I was riding. Sheriff Howard nabbed a couple of boys in town. He's a sly old fox. Had those boys thinking about being hung and Yuma and all kinds of unpleasantness before they told their story. Said they were innocent riders picked up to do a job of work but then found out the job was stealing and driving horses including some from the Circle S pasture. Thought you might want to know that you have a few animals heading towards Utah and Nevada."

Sam looked startled. "Well, you might say that's something we would want to know alright. Come in and we'll tell Pa and Benjamin. Pa will want to lift his Winchester off the hooks over the door and saddle up. He'll do it without too much thought. Benjamin's always able to settle him down till we lay out a plan. Ma just called that lunch was on the table. You might just as well have a bite while you're here."

In the house, I shook hands with Bob and Ben and said 'hello' to Mrs. Stanton. Sam introduced me to Sophie, his wife. We all sat to the table and while we were dishing up, Sam told the family about the thefts.

Sam was right about his father. Bob bolted right up out of his chair and headed for the door, his meal forgotten, before Sam had the story half out. Ben laughed a bit and said, "Settle down, Pa. That bunch has been gone two days. No point in rushing off without a plan. Let's figure this thing out. Finish our lunch, too."

Sam then told about the C/R losing stock and that brought a laugh and a shake of Bob's head. "Well, we had better all go and help old Ransom. He's so old he can't hardly set a horse so he'll need some help. And when he gets angry, which is most of the time, he can't hardly think or see straight.

"We'll be gone a spell. You boys put some gear together. Ma, I'd admire if you could rustle up some trail supplies. I'll go and rope out some horses." He started to get up again.

Benjamin put his hand on his father's arm. "Whoa, Pa. That's not a plan. We need to think this thing out better than that. We still have a ranch to care for and womenfolk here, and Sam has a youngster to be concerned about. I'd suggest that Sam and I go after the horses and you stay here to care for things, Pa. You're as old as Ransom and it might be hard on you, riding for days on end." I thought I saw the start of a grin on Sam's face and Mrs. Stanton looked at the table and quietly said, "My, my."

The explosion was totally predictable even though I didn't know these folks. Stanton got up so fast he tipped his chair over onto the floor. He was so angry he was sputtering. I don't know that I ever met a man so quick to anger. "I'll be still riding while you two are begging for mercy. Old, is it? I've ridden trails…"

He was drowned out by the laughter around the table. Even Mrs. Stanton's shoulders were shaking although she never lifted her eyes off the table. Benjamin finally quit laughing and said, "Sit down, Pa. I'm just ribbing you a bit."

He looked over at Sam. "What would y'all think if Pa and I were to saddle up? You stay here and care for things, Sam. I don't like the thought of us all leaving with just the women left here.

"I don't expect we'll be gone more than a few days. We'll get the horses and head right back, always assuming that I can keep Pa and Ransom from butting heads."

There was a general murmur of assent around the table. Bob got up and walked out the door, stuffing another piece of chocolate cake into his mouth as he went.

Benjamin said, "Sam, could you fetch some saddlebags and a couple of canvas panniers and help Ma pack up some grub and a coffeepot and such? Put a few boxes of extra cartridges aside, too. Our old bedrolls are still rolled up under the stairs so I'll get them and help Pa ready the horses. It's cold of a night, Ma, so an extra blanket each would be welcome. It's late in the day for riding but there's no way Pa's going to sit by until morning. Maybe you could find time too, Sam, to see about fixing the pasture fence."

In surprisingly short time, Ben and his father were

saddled and riding, leading a well-loaded packhorse behind. The dog barked them out of the yard and they were soon out of sight.

I made my good-byes and rode back to the H-R where I couldn't find a polite way to refuse another cup of coffee while I brought them up to date on the actions at the Circle S. Hamilton rode with me far enough to show me the shortcut through the hills and in no time at all I was back home.

Dora came running out of the house. "My goodness, I was just thinking something awful must have happened, like maybe you had decided you didn't like being married after all and had run off." She gasped all of that out between welcoming kisses, ending with, "Where did you find the horse?"

I told her the whole story over coffee and fresh bread still warm from the oven. A jar of strawberry spread was open on the table before us, a gift brought to the wedding by some neighbor. It was amazing how much coffee I was able to drink when there was a bit of home-baking to go with it.

25

NARRATOR

THE CIRCLE S riders cut across hills and through some light forest, taking the shortest backcountry route to the C/R. They rode into the ranch yard in time to see a flurry of activity. Or at least as much of a flurry as one horse and a lone man could make. A woman was standing by, her hands on her ample hips.

Clark Ransom was in the pole corral trying to control a half-wild-looking black. The horse was dancing and stomping on the end of the rope, its eyes rolled back in it head, its shuffling feet filling the corral with dust and frightened shrieks while the man filled the air with promises of evil things that would befall the animal if it didn't settle down. There didn't seem to be much give in either combatant.

The Stanton's, father and son both, almost laughed out loud when the test of wills finally settled into a foolish tug-of-war, the man with his big-heeled boots dug into the filth of the corral and the animal with its feet planted. Both were pulling full out on the rope.

Bob Stanton rode up to the corral and from the safety of distance, spoke into the silence that had finally descended over the scene, "If that little set-to was a contest to decide which of you is the brightest, my vote would go to the horse."

Ransom eased up on the rope and whirled around. "By all that's holy, Stanton, what're you doing here? Ain't I got enough to do without I got to figure some way to get rid of unwanted Texans?"

Bob Stanton pushed his hat back a bit on his head and looked over at his son. "Ben, now here's a lesson on how not to run a ranch. We got horse thieves ransacking the countryside making off with the Circle S remuda and a bunch of C/R broomtails and Ransom just lets it all happen while he practices his dance moves with a half-broke black mustang. Still, it takes all kinds, I guess. I suppose you and I might just as well go find us some rustlers and leave Ransom to his foolishness. I don't see any way that he's going to be much help to us."

Ransom dropped the rope and charged out of the corral. "Why you Texas bonehead, don't you think I know my horses have been stole? Why do you think I'm getting ready for the trail? There's not a man living who can claim to have ever stole a thing from the C/R without they were caught and paid a price. The couple who thought they could do it are in boot hill. Just as quick as I get saddled up I'll track the thieves down and they'll be sorry they ever rode into Colorado. You can go home to your rocking chair if you want. I'll bring your nags back first chance I get."

Bob Stanton just couldn't resist another jab at his cantankerous neighbor. "I expect we'll have the thieves caught before you ever get a saddle on that black, you've worked him into such a frenzy. It's a good thing you ain't running the army. We'd be at war with each other again and never know why."

Ransom spit a brown gob onto the ground beside Stanton's horse, his voice getting louder each time he spoke. "Army, is it? I been in the danged army, you fool. Done my part, too. Most of which it's best to forget except that sometimes of a night it all comes back. Don't you be talking no army talk with me.

"Now, what do you know about these horse thieves? I just found my fence cut this morning and about a dozen head missing that I plan to get back. Took my best riding animals and I'm left with this fool black and a couple of others that are maybe worse. There's a wagon team in the barn but they ain't no riding animals."

While this loud exchange was taking place, Mrs. Ransom walked into the corral, slipped the rope off the black and with a gentle tug on his halter, quietly led the animal out, tying it to the corral rail beside an already loaded packhorse.

Ben stepped out of the saddle and went over to the black. He stroked it on the neck and spoke to Mrs. Ransom. "That's a good looking horse. Maybe needs a little riding to take the ginger out of it but a nice horse just the same."

Mrs. Ransom nodded in agreement. "Clark is actually quite a good horseman. But he got so upset when he saw that fence cut and the other animals gone that he kind of lost control of himself. Scared that poor black half to death. Don't you be judging him too harshly. He's never abused an animal. He demands more of himself than he does of his horses."

His father and Ransom were discussing horse thieves

again and their voices were even louder than they were before.

Ben pointed at some gear draped over the top rail of the corral. "Is this Clark's saddle"

At Mrs. Ransom's quiet 'yes', he swung the rig off the rail and onto the back of the black. The saddlebags came next and then the bridle. He coiled the rope and tied it to the saddle horn.

As he was saddling the black, Ben said, "Met your son and his family at the wedding. You must enjoy having them around."

Mrs. Ransom showed her first small smile. "It's good to have them. Clark has trouble saying 'thanks' or asking for help but he knows he couldn't have run the ranch much longer alone. Getting old is scaring both of us more than we want to admit. Having Hank home is a godsend. And, of course, I'm enjoying getting to know Sarah and the kids."

Ben was trying to think of a polite way to ask if Hank would be joining the horse hunters when Mrs. Ransom said, "Hank and Sarah took the wagon to town last evening. A few hours alone will do them good and I enjoy caring for the kids. I had a long list of things we needed from the store. I looked for them to be home before this. I expect they'll be along shortly."

When the animal was rigged out and tied to the corral railing, Mrs. Ransom smiled, nodded and walked up to the house, saying nothing at all to her still shouting husband.

As Ben watched her walk away, he was remembering this woman taking charge at the town dances and again at the Gates wedding. She didn't seem like the same person. All he could think of was that this had all happened before and she was content to let the situation resolve itself.

Ben stepped into the saddle, tugging his own packhorse along as he headed out of the yard. He grabbed the reins of his father's horse as he rode past. Big Bob and Clark Ransom were still arguing. At the movement of his horse, Big Bob grabbed for the saddle horn and reached for the reins that were no longer there. He hollered at Ben, "Let a-go of my reins. What do you think you're doing?"

"I'm going horse-thief hunting, Pa. You can come along or go home but make up your mind. I'm leaving now." He dropped the reins and Big Bob had to bend far forward, scrambling to grab them before the horse stepped on them.

Clark Ransom watched them ride off and then turned around to find his horse rigged out and ready to ride. Seeming to have forgotten the tussle in the corral and giving not a thought to how the animal happened to be rigged out, he swung aboard, picked up the lead rope for the packhorse and moved across his own ranch yard. His wife was watching from the kitchen window but he didn't look that way or notice her.

Ransom put his animals into an easy trot and moved to get in front of the two Stanton riders, showing himself to be the leader, but pulled up when a new group of riders turned in at his gate.

Noah lifted his hand in a short greeting. "Mr. Ransom, we met at the wedding a few weeks ago. Hello again, Bob, Ben. I'm supposing you all know the Abner family." He nodded his head towards the three men riding beside him.

Abner spoke up, "Ain't much fer neighbor'n. Know Ransom. Don't know these others."

Noah said, "Mr. Abner, this is Bob and Ben Stanton from the Circle S over east a ways. They lost some horses, too. Bob, Ben, this is Enoch, Ephraim and Caleb. They didn't lose any stock but when I went by their place to ask their daughter Laura to go stay with Dora while I was away, they insisted on coming along." He turned to the Abner riders. "Again men, I appreciate your help."

"Never did hold with standing by while others were in need. Me and the boys, we'll tag along."

Ransom reluctantly said, "Welcome, men. I don't suppose we really need help but you just never know."

Ben gave Ransom a troubled look and shook his head. Big Bob rode closer and shook hands with the Abner men and said, "Appreciate the help." Ben then rode over and shook hands.

Big Bob turned to Noah. "Didn't know you had lost stock, Gates. You didn't mention it out at the ranch."

"I didn't. In fact I gained one animal. One of the men the sheriff cornered in town was riding a horse of mine that was stolen over a year ago. I figure I'll just ride along and see if the gang has any more of my G-bar animals. Anyway, I always set out to be neighborly when opportunity provides. And I haven't got one single thing that needs doing on the G-bar so it's good to find a reason to ride out."

Ransom, tired of the talk, kicked his black into motion. "We're burn'n daylight."

Ben grinned at Noah and swung in beside him as they moved out.

Night's darkness found the searchers in a small valley dotted with aspens and a scattering of spruce. They were still a half-day's ride from the Poudre. Clark Ransom pulled his horses into a small cul-de-sac with a good growth of grass and a small running stream. "Can't see to follow tracks no more. Might just as well roll out our bedding and make coffee." He hobbled his animals and started gathering dried branches for building a fire.

A tasteless meal was put together with the fixings the men were able to pull from their packs in the dark and they were soon bedded down, taking turns standing guard. Somehow the evening had turned into night without Ransom and Stanton setting at each other again.

The night passed without interruption and, after drinking coffee and eating cold biscuits brought from home, the men were saddled and moving before full light. Enoch Abner joined Ransom as they led the group out. The hoof-churned grass left a trail that was easily followed but one of the Abner boys had said over coffee, "Pa could do some scout'n if'n y'all wished. Given need, I believe he could follow a snake over a flat rock." No one commented but when they lifted to their saddles, Enoch moved to the front. No one challenged him.

26

NARRATOR

HANK AND SARAH RANSOM arrived home from their trip into Canyon View in mid-afternoon. They drove the loaded wagon in a circle in front of the ranch house and stopped beside the walkway leading to the kitchen door. Hanna Ransom opened the door and the two little boys ran out hollering 'hellos' to their parents.

Hank stepped to the ground and tousled the hair on Zeke's head while Sarah picked Toby up and hugged him, whirling him around in a circle. "Were you good for Grandma?"

Toby was trying to find his youthful words when Zeke shouted out, "Grandpa went chasing some bad men who stole our horses."

Hank's head jerked up at this statement. He looked at his mother still standing on the back porch. "What's that about stolen horses?"

Hanna stepped down onto the sidewalk. "Let's get these supplies into the house and I'll tell you all about it."

A half-hour later, the wagon was unloaded and the team turned into the pasture. The three adults sat at the kitchen table with hot coffee and a loaf of fresh-baked bread sitting in front of them. Hanna told what she knew. "I don't know who the thieves are or how many horses they took. Noah Gates was here. He said the thieves were called the Barger gang. I've never heard that name before and can't tell you any more than I've already said."

Hank stirred his coffee and looked out the window as if he was trying to make a decision. "Who all rode out?"

His mother named off the neighbors that had ridden with the group while Hank continued to study the back-yard garden. Noah was the only man he really knew. He had met some of the others at the wedding but couldn't have named them. He was glad his father was not alone. His father had always been one who was either shooting or shouting. Thinking came later, if it ever came at all. He had been mixed up in a world of trouble at one time or another.

Hank felt it was somehow unjust that he would be the one to end up in prison. He had always been urging caution on his father and had looked for the peaceful way. And yet a simple barroom fight had robbed a man of his life and Hank of three years of his freedom. He would never live down the shame. These thoughts all roared through his head as he tried to think what to do. The remembrance of the prison at Santa Fe and the thought of returning there caused chills to run up his spine. But he knew he had to do something about the stolen horses if he was to be considered a man to be trusted and respected by his neighbors.

Finally, he stood up. "I'd best harness the other team

and ready the wagon. Anyone gets hurt out there they'll have to be hauled back. I was really hoping to never again be involved in anything like this but, with Pa the way he is, it's bound to happen."

His mother immediately came to her husband's defense. "You can't expect a man to have his horses stolen and sit idly by while the thieves ride away."

"That's true, Ma. I know it full well. But Pa has been a lightning rod for trouble all his born days. I know he didn't ask to have thieves hit our ranch but what he'll do when he finds the thieves is what worries me. You can't just up and hang a man any more. Those days are past but I doubt as how Pa understands that."

His mother had no response.

"Sarah, if you could pull my bedroll out of that closet and add a change of clothes, I'll hitch up the wagon. I'll throw in a layer of hay, too, in case someone needs to be toted home."

Hank wheeled the wagon back to the kitchen door. He stepped down and loaded the bedroll Sarah handed him and then went into the house for his carbine. His Colt was already in place, belted and holstered on his hip. He kissed his wife and again tousled Zeke's hair and then did the same to Toby. He spoke to his mother, "What's your best guess about where they headed out to?"

Hanna stood on the porch, her arms wrapped around her waist. She had watched her men ride out many times but somehow she had never gotten used to the sight. "All I know is that the animals were taken from the south pasture and the men turned that way when they left the yard. Where they went after that I have no idea."

Hank turned the wagon south at the end of the ranch road and followed the large group of horse tracks that headed that way.

27

NARRATOR

HAVING SPENT several weeks following and mapping the highest points of land, the small army troop with their novice mapping crew was ready to find their way out of the hills, their task of mapping the Great Divide completed for their assigned section. They weren't the first to tackle this task. It was a training exercise for their mapping division and a way of checking the data compiled by others.

Sergeant Galligan lifted his right hand to stop the troop and rode back from his scout position to speak to Lieutenant Bradley. "Sir, there's a promising little river just ahead. It flows in the bottom of a considerable valley but this canyon we're in leads right into it. Best I can tell, it's heading mostly east although the way these hills and valleys twist around it might fool us. But it's the best we've seen. The valley ain't too wide and we may have to take to the water at times but I'm suggesting we try it. If we're wishing to head east, this seems like a chance at least."

Lieutenant Bradley thought for no more than a few seconds. "Lead on, Sergeant. If we have to make a correction later, we will." He turned to the map crew. "Take note of this river valley, men. We don't have time to be doing a formal survey so just draw it as accurately as you can as we go along."

The sergeant led the troop down a steep, rocky slope. Each step of his horse's iron shoes announced his coming. He dropped into the narrow river valley and turned downstream. Within a short distance, he came upon a large grass-covered clearing in a bend of the river. Allowing his horse to stop for a drink, he waited for the troop to catch up. "How would you feel about a noon rest for the animals, sir?"

"Give the order, Sergeant."

The men dismounted, loosened saddle girths and turned their horses out to graze and drink. There was no easy way out of the valley and with a man posted at either end of the clearing, the animals were freed.

Lieutenant Bradley stretched, relieving a pain in his back and then looked around the little copse of grass and trees, their leaves all golden and shimmering in the sunlight. "This is a uniquely beautiful little valley, Sergeant. You could find trees that are more magnificent in their size and grandeur but nothing pleases the eye more than the quaking aspen when they are all golden in the fall of the year, their leaves rustling with the slightest breeze. A truly restful place.

"But our task is not to find a restful place so instruct the men to take their ease for thirty minutes. Then mount up, ready to move out. We'll hope to be somewhere in the vicinity of Fort Collins in the next day or two if this valley truly does lead us out of the mountains."

"Yes, sir."

The sergeant saw no need for shouted orders in the calm of the little copse of trees so when the thirty minutes had passed, he simply stepped into his saddle, quietly said, "Mount up," and took the lead following the river downstream. The clattering of hooves on rock and the clanging of the troop's accouterments signaled that the men were following. Before long, the troop was forced into the water as the canyon narrowed and the steep rock walls and overhanging trees put the area into shadow. Nowhere was the water deeper than halfway up the horse's legs. They had ridden perhaps three miles, alternating between the water and the narrow river bank, leaving the water as opportunity offered. There was no chance of hiding their progress as iron-shod hooves clattered on rock.

The sound of their own march drowned out the sounds of horses coming upstream. Suddenly, without warning, a rider rounded a bend ahead of them. Following the rider were several more herders spread along both river banks and, between the riders, a large herd of driven horses.

Surprised by seeing other riders in the river valley, Sergeant Galligan pulled rein and lifted his hand to halt the troop. The drover facing him was startled into a sudden stop also. The horses and undisciplined drovers following behind became a milling, water-thrashing mix of riders and driven animals.

Lieutenant Bradley rode forward at the sergeant's signal. "What's happening, Serg...?"

He was interrupted by a rifle shot coming from downstream. The lieutenant clutched his shoulder, trying to stifle a groan as his pain-filled eyes rolled back into his head. He slid from the saddle into the shallow water. His horse shied and turned back into the gathered troops, causing chaos with the other horses. The troops were pulling their rifles and frantically looking around for targets. The sergeant pulled his sidearm and took sight on one of the drovers who was aiming a rifle at the troop. He was too far away for effective shooting with the handgun from the back of a stamping horse but he did manage to distract the shooter. A couple of troopers had more success. The crashing of weapons echoed off the canyon walls. One horse and two riders floated away on the rushing water through a tangle of horse's legs, causing even more chaos among the drovers. Within a few seconds, the drovers had fallen back behind a bend of the river and out of sight. The terrified horses broke into a wild run, some turning back and some charging, river water splashing in every direction into the army position.

As the drovers disappeared, Sergeant Galligan held up his right arm still holding his pistol. "Cease firing, cease firing. Dismount and form up for defense. Get the surgeon up here." He then stepped down and assisted the struggling lieutenant out of the water. The officer's left shoulder was bleeding freely and his eyes were glazed with pain.

At the tail end of the drive, several drovers had turned and were making their way back downstream as fast as they could, pushing a few horses before them with other terrified animals pushing from behind. The water, rocks and trees impeded their progress.

Phil Barger had yet to clear the curve in the canyon wall. He had not seen where the shooting had come from. He hollered at Mason Benson, his second in command who had been leading the drive, "What happened? Who's shooting at us?"

Benson turned in his saddle and shouted back, "The army. Blue coats. What in all tarnation is the army doing up here?"

Barger was angry beyond reason. "Which one of our men fired that first shot? I'll skin him alive, causing all this.

It's just stupid to shoot at the army. They're not looking for us."

"Adams fired that shot, boss, but it's too late to skin him. That's him floating around the bend down there."

Barger called Benson over beside him. "You try to get the drive sorted out while I talk with the army." With that he holstered his sidearm and kicked his horse forward, holding his hands up at shoulder height. As he came in sight of the army position, he saw twenty or so rifles pointed his way while a small group of men hunched over a downed rider.

He kept riding slowly forward. "Sorry for that misunderstanding, men," he shouted. "I hope there's no one bad hurt over here. The man who fired that first shot is down. One of you killed him. I don't know what he was thinking but I didn't give any order to start a fracas. All we need to do is drive our remuda past your position and we can both go about our business."

Sergeant Galligan stood and turned toward Barger. "Ride forward and dismount. Do it slowly."

When Barger was standing on the ground, Galligan motioned to a trooper standing close by. "Private, lift his sidearm and lead his animal away." Turning to Barger, he said, "Now explain yourself, mister. Make it plain and fast. You can see that the lieutenant took one of your shots. We're in no mood for foolishness."

Barger half turned and motioned back towards where Mason had gathered up a few of the milling horses and shouting drovers. "We're horse traders moving this herd to the western states. Got a contract for supply to the miners in Utah and Nevada. The last thing we might have expected was to run into anyone else in this remote valley let alone the army. I can't explain why one of my men got excited and took that shot. It certainly wasn't on my orders. But I can tell you that man is shot dead and floating down the river along with another man and a horse.

"I don't have any medical supplies with me beyond a few cloths for bandages so I can't offer much help to your lieutenant. But I see that he's getting good care so, if you wished, we could just drive past and we could all go about our business."

Another flurry of shots echoed from down the river followed by a jumble of muted shouts. Barger and Galligan both turned their eyes that way and almost in unison said, "Now, what's that all about?"

Sgt. Galligan shouted at the troopers, "Fall back to that copse we just passed, back upstream. Form up for defense. A couple of you men give a hand here with the lieutenant."

As the green troops were milling about, some near panic, they caught up their own animals and rode back to where the troop was gathering, leaving the stolen remuda behind.

Barger took the opportunity to swing aboard his big red stallion, ducking under some sheltering aspens and around a small bend. He was soon out of sight, driving the loose horses before him.

Within minutes, he caught up to Benson who had stationed himself on a little river bank. "Benson," he shouted. "What's going on now? Who's doing the shooting?"

Benson hollered back across the river, "Don't know. But I see another of our men down. Could be that some of those ranchers are on our trail. Whoever it is, they're getting closer judging by the shooting and the shouting. I don't see any good end to this, Phil. I think you and I had better duck out of sight and wait it out, see what happens. Horses ain't worth dying for."

The loose horses continued downstream, a few in the

water and several on the narrow bank. Clark Ransom and Bob Stanton moved to the side of the small river and held their horses steady while the charging remuda swept past them. A short ways behind them Noah Gates pushed his animal into the bush to avoid the running horses.

Barger thought for just a moment, looking around. Ever one to think of himself first, he gave no consideration at all to his men and the fight they were in. "Let's have a look at that side canyon. But do it quick. There's no time to lose."

Benson's horse made a hard job of getting out of the water, up the rocky edge and into the tree-shrouded side canyon with Barger close on his heels. The clattering of their horses' hooves on the rocks was loud, announcing where they rode, but they couldn't do anything about it. As quickly as the conditions allowed, they inched under over-hanging shrubs and vines and through the undergrowth sheltering the little canyon. Barger was feeling safer as they moved forward.

Clark Ransom, riding beside Big Bob Stanton - the two of them determined to be at the front of the action - had pushed forward through the stolen horses. They were just in time to see the shrubbery swaying with the passage of Barger's horse and then they saw the horse itself just as it disappeared into the undergrowth.

Forgetting his rivalry with Big Bob for a moment and intent on catching the rustlers, Ransom pointed to his left. "Up there. They're gone up that side cut." He pointed his horse up the rocky bank and into the bush, paying no attention to whether Bob was following or not. But Bob was following right behind using his Winchester to push the bush in front of him aside.

Downstream, the ranchers caught or gunned down what was left of the rustlers, firmly tying the two survivor's hands behind their backs. Ben Stanton rode up to Enoch Abner. "Mr. Abner, I'd like if you were to take charge of these two rustlers and the herd. Push them right out of this valley and onto open ground and wait for the rest of us. We'll decide what's to be done when we're all together."

Abner saw no reason for talk and simply called his son, "Ephraim, round up those loose horses and bring them along." He then pointed his carbine towards the rustlers. "I could shoot y'all now or hang ya later. You might get another couple of hours of life if you ride slowly down the river. Up to you."

The men turned their horses downstream and Enoch followed. Ephraim rounded up the loose horses and started the long, ten-mile push to where the river emerged from the canyon. Arriving at the canyon's mouth, they gathered the animals on a level, grassy plain. Hank Ransom was just arriving with the wagon.

Ben Stanton saw where his father had left the river and hollered at Caleb Abner. "Pa and Ransom went off to the left. They must have seen something. I'm going after them. Come along if you wish."

Caleb and Ben were making their way through the rushing river, their eyes fixed on the break in the bush where Big Bob and Ransom had gone, when the army swept around a narrow bend pushing the remaining stolen horses before them. There was no space on either side of the river for Caleb and Ben to climb out. They had no choice but to turn and go downstream ahead of the army.

NARRATOR

BARGER AND BENSON made it only about a quarter-mile up the side canyon before the way was blocked by heavy forest and fallen rock at the end of a one-acre clearing with steep canyon walls beyond. Frantically Barger whirled his horse in a circle looking for a way out. There were no trails leading off and there was no chance at all of escape up the steep canyon walls. Perhaps a man on foot could clamber his way from tree to tree and make the top but he would still be nowhere when he got there with no escape possible. There was forest and steep hillsides and more rock everywhere they looked.

Benson was frantic, riding his horse from one end of the little clearing to another and then back again. He looked over at Barger, stark terror in his eyes. "We've bought it this time, Phil. There ain't no gettin' out of here."

They could hear the clang of iron-shod hooves on rock. Every hoof-fall brought the sound closer. Knowing there was no time left for finding a way out, Barger pointed at a cluster of fallen rock at the end of the cul-de-sac. "There; it's our best chance. Grab your extra ammunition and your canteen and get behind those rocks. It's too fine a day to be dying. Hunker down and keep quiet."

Without even thinking what he was doing, Benson looked around him at the trees with the sunlight slanting through the branches and glittering off the fall-colored leaves. He took note of the autumn-browned grass, the blue sky overhead with just a single gray cloud visible between the peaks of the hillsides. It was a fine country. The horse felt good under him and his body was full of life. It was far too fine a day to be dying. But he also had known this day would come. He never went on a raid but what he wondered if he would return or if he would lay bloody and broken in the dust like he had seen so many others. His mind took on a path of its own and an immense sadness came over him. He admitted to himself that, for all the money the gang had stolen, the average ranch cowboy lived a better life than he had, running and hiding and living in fear.

Benson jerked his head around when he heard Barger shout, "Move!" He kicked his horse in the direction of the rocks Barger was crawling behind. He jumped off his horse, grabbing his carbine and canteen. He wasted a few seconds untying his saddlebags but finally he and Barger were both hidden behind the cluster of rock. They left the horses running loose although there was really nowhere for them to go. Barger ordered, "Stay down and keep quiet until we see the situation. We may get out of this yet."

Ransom and Stanton burst into the clearing. They immediately saw the two loose horses but had no idea where the men they were following had hidden themselves. Ransom fearlessly rode his horse towards the end of the clearing while Stanton scouted along the northerly edge. As Ransom came close to the thieves' hideout, Benson lost his nerve. He jumped to his knees behind the rocks and lifted his carbine, his action mostly hidden by brush.

"No," whispered Barger frantically but it was too late. Benson drew a quick bead on Clark Ransom and pulled the trigger. He had hoped for a killing shot but, in his haste, he had aimed quickly and badly. The shot tore into Ransom's thigh and continued through into the stomach of the horse. Ransom cried out and leaned forward gripping the saddle horn, his eyes tearing from the pain. The animal screamed out in shock and agony; the horse ran uncontrolled to the other side of the clearing before going to its knees. Ransom went over the horse's head and landed in a heap in a growth of willows.

At the sound of the shot, Bob Stanton whirled his horse around in time to see Ransom's horse run and then stagger and fall. He watched helplessly as Ransom flew over the horse's head. He charged across the clearing until he was close to where Ransom lay and then pulled his horse to a sliding stop, the bit a cruel message in its mouth. Forgetting his age for a moment, Stanton leaped off his horse and went to his knees. He dropped his carbine and was reaching for it when two shots ricocheted off the grass beside him. His horse ran off in fear, joining the two animals that Barger and Benson had turned loose. The three animals were heading, stirrups flopping, for the trail to the river.

Stanton frantically grabbed the fallen gun and dove into the willow bush that Ransom's horse had pitched him into. Ransom was huddled behind a small rock, his clothing covered in dirt, dead leaves and blood. He was trying to tie his bandana around his leg for a tourniquet.

Stanton lay flat, sprawled behind some rock. He adjusted his hat which he had come close to losing and spat some grass and dirt out of his mouth. "You old fool, you went and got yourself shot." When Ransom didn't answer, Stanton asked, "How bad is it?"

Ransom never seemed to let up on his long-time difference with Stanton. "Ain't no problem at all. I've got another leg I can use."

Stanton looked at the old man and shook his head. After looking around a bit, he said, "We ain't safe here. I'm going to drag you behind that bigger circle of rocks over there. It would help if you could control your tongue while I do it."

Without any more warning, Stanton stood in a crouch and grabbed Ransom's two arms. Ransom held a desperate grasp on his carbine. Taking a tight grip on the man's wrists, he backed as fast as he could across a few feet of grass and brush and into a cluster of rocks. His carbine was flopping under his arm but he managed to hold it. A few shots followed the two men. When Ransom was lying behind the rocks, Stanton started rolling more rocks into place to reinforce their hideout. He then untied the bandana from Ransom's leg and retied it with a short stick inserted in the wrap. He twisted the stick until Ransom cried out in pain. "I know that hurts, old timer, but the bleeding's slowing down."

"Who you calling old? I'll be here still baying at the moon when you're sitting on a rocker with a blanket over your knees."

Stanton took a cautious look around a rock, studying where the shots had come from. "Well, that might all be true, but right now we just need to stay alive and there's a couple of men hidden over there who are trying to see that doesn't happen. I can see where they are. If you thought you could close your mouth for a while and pick up your rifle to cover me, I'm going to climb that bank behind us. There's been a rock slide there some time ago. I believe it'll give a clear look down into that cluster of boulders the thieves are behind. I'll circle around a bit to get some cover in the trees and I should be able to shoot right down into their hideout."

Ransom nodded his agreement. He tried to roll over to get a better look at where the two fugitives were hiding but cried out in pain at the movement and gave it up. Twisting his body as far as his wounded leg would allow, he finally got his weapon aimed in the direction of the two horse thieves. He fired three quick shots off the rocks the thieves were hidden behind. "OK, go."

With that Stanton rushed, crouching over, into the thick brush behind their rocky alcove. He worked his way to the side until he thought he would be out of sight and started his way up, pulling himself from tree to tree. Within a couple of minutes, he was able to look right down into the thieves' hideout. He struggled for a moment with the idea of shouting a warning or asking for surrender but finally decided on a warning shot. He went to one knee with the other leg placed carefully on a rock wedged into the top of the cut bank created by the previous landslide and hidden by more brush.

He raised the carbine to his shoulder and leaned forward for a better sighting, shifting his weight onto the rock. The rock gave way and Big Bob Stanton tumbled forward rolling over and over down the bank followed by a large gathering of dirt, rocks and dislodged brush.

Ransom, lying below the cut bank, just had time to protect his head with his folded arms. Rock and dirt and gravel piled all around him and partially buried his legs. A great cloud of dust hid the rest of the world from his view.

29

NOAH

I NOSED off the trail and into the bush just in time to allow several running horses to sweep past me; then the army rode past pushing the rest of the loose remuda. When I backed my horse out onto the small trail again, I saw Stanton and Ransom pushing their animals into a side canyon. They were a good quarter-mile upstream from my position. I followed. Just as I reached the side canyon, I heard shots.

Two terrified horses raced past me and charged into the running water of the river, leaping over the three-foot drop from the trail. And then a third charged out of the bush, nearly knocking me over as he entered the river. One horse was a big red stallion that sure looked like my G-bar animal that was stolen the year before. I didn't have time to worry about it right at that moment though.

I ran my horse as fast as I could through the trees and scattered rock until I broke into a clearing. I pulled up there to look around. I was just in time to see Bob Stanton fly into midair and then fall head first onto the steep hillside and roll end over end, swallowed up in a small avalanche of rock and dirt. A startled cry of alarm that I guessed would be from Clark Ransom was absorbed in the thunder of the landslide. A cloud of dust obscured the two men.

The two thieves broke from cover. Obviously thinking this was their chance at escape, they ran towards Ransom and Stanton, firing their Winchesters from the hip. I saw nothing of Bob Stanton but, as the dust cleared enough to see a bit, Ransom, covered in dust and debris from the slide, poked his carbine over the lip of a rock and returned fire as quickly as he could work the lever.

One thief dropped his weapon and went to his knees, holding his stomach with his wrapped arms. The next shot from Ransom hit the man in the chest. He fell sideways and didn't move. The second thief cut quickly to his right, attempting to get a clear shot around the end of the rock barrier Stanton and Ransom were huddled behind.

The thief hadn't seen me as I ran my horse across the clearing. I was praying that Ransom wouldn't mistake me for one of the horse thieves. As the thief ran dodging Ransom's bullets, I hollered, "Hold your fire." I drove my horse into the desperate, running man. The impact knocked him several feet through the air. He crumpled to the ground and lay there unconscious as I pulled my horse to a stop.

As I turned my horse back towards the rock hideout, Ransom pulled himself partially onto the rock. A moment later, Stanton came to his knees and then sat down on the biggest rock in the circle. His hat was gone, his shirt was torn and he was covered in dirt. He was bleeding from a cut on his forehead and he looked a little glassy-eyed.

Ransom called over to me, "Well done, young feller." Pointing at the crumpled form on the ground, he said, "Now if you were to put a bullet where it counts, we'd have about wrapped this shindig up."

I rode my horse to where the two men were sitting on the rocks. "I believe we'll call it done for now. Putting a bullet into anyone is no part of my plan. Other than being on the receiving end of an avalanche, are either of y'all hurt?"

Ransom hooked his thumb over at Big Bob. "Bad enough I went and got myself shot in the leg. This fool Texan went and brought the whole danged mountain down on us. Ain't no hope for some folks. But we're alive and the thieves ain't. For the most part, anyway. The boys will have our horses gathered up so I guess you could say it all turned out alright. I ain't never going to turn my back on a Texan again though."

Big Bob just shook his head until the pain of a fierce headache and a twisted knee forced him to stop. "Old man, if you could raise cattle with your mouth you'd be the richest cattleman anywhere around. Now my head hurts from conking it on that rock and my knee is about ready to have me screaming in misery. Beyond that, every bone in my body hurts. My ears are about the only thing that doesn't hurt and you're about to spoil that. How about you see how quiet you can be till we get out of here?"

I stepped off my horse and tied him to a willow. He was the only animal we had left and to get Ransom and Stanton out of here the gelding would have to carry double. I didn't want to think of the mess we'd be in without the horse.

I went to the downed thief and wrapped his dead partner's belt around his arms, tying them securely behind his back. He was showing signs of life so I kicked him in the ribs and said, "Get up. You get up and stand still. I've got a partner here who wants to put a bullet in you just on general principles. I've stopped him for now but you try to run away and you can expect three of us pulling the trigger."

The man struggled to stand without the use of his hands but he finally made it. He stood glaring at the three of us. "Well, you win, but we made you hurt a bit anyway." Ransom lifted his Winchester but before he swung it around on the thief, Stanton reached and pulled the weapon down. "No more," is all he said.

I led the horse over to the circle of rocks and passed the reins to Ransom to hold. I then helped Bob Stanton to his feet. He was a big man and it was a struggle to get him into the saddle but once I lifted his foot into the stirrup and gave him a push, he was able to do the rest himself. He had to mount from the off side because of his twisted knee. Raising that damaged knee over the horse and settling down in the saddle took all the grit the man had in him.

I took the reins from Ransom and passed them to Big Bob. He held the gelding steady while I lifted Clark Ransom up behind the saddle. With the bullet in his leg he couldn't do much more than grab Bob's offered arm and hold on while I lifted. The old man wasn't much more than bone and gristle so I was able to handle his weight without too much trouble although he cried out in pain when his leg fell against the side of the horse.

I passed each man his carbine and waited while they reloaded. Big Bob pulled his Colt and gave it a quick cleaning, removing the dust that had gathered as he rolled down the hill.

Looking over at the thief, I said, "You lead out. You have three Winchesters aimed at you. You make one false move and you're going to spoil a perfectly nice afternoon. I'd hate to have to shoot you but I will. So will my two friends. You do your best to remember that. Now, let's go."

On foot, I followed the captured thief out of the side canyon. I led the horse and carried my carbine. In spite of my threats that the thief had three Winchesters aimed at him, I doubted the truth of the matter. Ransom and Stanton were all in, hurting and bleeding. I doubted if they would be much help in a confrontation.

We had to walk in the water once we were out of the side canyon but downstream a ways the canyon widened out enough so's we could climb to the river bank. We walked for two hours down that river valley, walking on the bank where it was possible and wading in the river when it was necessary. The water was cold and my feet and legs were becoming numb.

Then some of the boys met us, leading spare horses. A half-dozen troopers rode along with them. They were a welcome sight and we soon had Clark Ransom lifted onto another animal.

We placed the captured thief bareback on a roan gelding. Ephraim Abner threw a loop over the gelding's neck and led off with the thief gripping the animal with his knees. Ephraim showed not the slightest sign of mercy. I stepped onto my own gelding.

I spoke to the troopers, "Men, how would you like to take another spare horse and go pick up that downed man? There will be some weapons dropped here and there, too. And maybe you can get the saddle off the dead horse. That would about wrap everything up on this end. You'll see the broken brush where we left the river if you watch on the left."

The corporal leading the group said simply, "Follow me, men."

By the time we joined the rest of our men, it was

coming on to dark. Ben Stanton and Hank Ransom had taken charge of caring for the horses. By looping saddle ropes together and stringing them from the few trees that grew on the river flat, they soon had a makeshift corral.

We turned our horses into the rope corral and changed into dry clothing from our packs. We huddled around the cooking fire, hoping to warm up before the cold of the mountain nighttime fell on us adding to our discomfort. The army had its own fires going and was preparing its suppers.

Enoch Abner and his two sons took charge of the prisoners. He had them sitting on the ground, their backs against the wagon tongue which Hank had dropped to the ground when he turned his team out to graze. Their arms were draped behind them and over the wagon tongue and then their wrists were firmly tied with a loop. They weren't going anywhere unless they were to drag the wagon with them.

I could see Abner talking to the prisoners. In a short while, he sauntered over to the fire and said, "The one on the far end is called 'Barger'. Seems to be the leader. I never heard of him before."

"I have," I said. "Apparently he's some big-time thief from back east. Banks, cattle, and - lately - horses. It appears as how he's the one that took my herd of trade animals almost two years ago. He's been at this for years. He'll know every trick. Watch he doesn't give us the slip."

Abner looked over at the tied men. "He ain't goin' nowhere."

Ben and Hank had spread out blankets from the wagon and were working over their fathers' injuries. Ben couldn't do much for Big Bob's twisted knee but he cleaned the dirt and blood off his head and arms and found a clean shirt for him stuffed in the bottom of a saddlebag. Big Bob was complaining that he had lost his hat and was all set to go look for it. Ben passed him a cup of coffee and said, "You got other hats."

Hank had heated water and was bathing Ransom's bullet wound. He looked up to the gathering at the fire and said, "Pa needs a doctor. It's coming to dark shortly but I'm thinking Ben and I should head to town anyway. We know the trail and Pa's wound shouldn't be let go. Mr. Stanton needs some doctoring, too."

30

NOAH

THE SERGEANT WALKED over to our fire and asked, "What are your plans, men? We're pulling out right away for Fort Collins. There's no military there anymore but there should be a doctor. The lieutenant needs medical help and I'm afraid morning might be too late although he's putting on a good front for the men."

We had been discussing Hank's suggestion of heading to Canyon View in spite of the darkness but no decision had been made. As the newcomer to the territory, it really wasn't my right to speak but before I had figured that out, I heard myself saying, "We're pulling out, too. The boys know the trail and we have two men that need doctoring; the sooner, the better."

No one argued with that and I saw a few nodding heads around the fire.

The sergeant looked over at the three men tied to the wagon tongue. "What about the prisoners?"

Ben spoke up, "We'll take them to the sheriff. They need hanging but that's beyond what our town sheriff can do. I expect he'll call in a Federal Marshall. Apparently, these boys have cut a wide swath across several states."

The sergeant nodded at Ben as if in agreement. But then he said, "It's not beyond what the army can do. I kind of figure that when these boys fired on the US Army and put a bullet in the lieutenant, they became guilty of treason. The army is pretty good at dealing with that. How would it be if you turn them over to me? I'll see that they're properly dealt with and your town man won't have to bother with it."

Clark Ransom, lying on the bloody blanket beside the fire said, "These Johnny-come-lately fellers won't let me deal with those three the way they should be dealt with. If you can guarantee that they won't escape and that they'll feel a rope or a bullet from a firing squad, I'll be glad to see the end of them."

There was a murmur of agreement around the fire.

The sergeant had detailed off a burial squad for the downed thieves. By the time they were done with the gristly chore, the troop was ready to hit their saddles.

I walked over to the sergeant. "I've spent many a month looking for my stolen G-bar horses. I see one of them in your remuda. Until today, I would have asked for him back but I think we'll just let it go. We'd have been in some trouble here today without you boys. Keep the animal as a part of my thanks."

The sergeant just nodded his head and said, "Saddle up, men."

The lieutenant looked worn and hurting in his saddle, but determined. His uniform jacket and pants were badly stained with blood. But he took his place beside the sergeant at the front of the column and said, "Move them out, Sergeant."

Watching his show of strength and duty, I figured he just might turn into a leader worthy of being followed.

A couple of tall, rail-thin troopers, both with cheeks bulging with chew, had taken charge of the prisoners. Enoch Abner watched as they trussed the thieves to their saddles. Nodding at the prison escort, he said to no one in particular, "Them there mountain boys ain't about to lose their prisoners."

Abner and his sons pushed the horses on ahead. "We'll corral them at the C/R. Y'all can sort them out another time."

The going was slow for the wagon. Hank tried to avoid the worst of the rough trail but with each bump and lurch of the wagon, Big Bob and Clark Ransom were bounced around. They had to be hurting in spite of the layer of hay they were lying on.

It was nearing midnight when we pulled into the C/R. The kitchen windows shone with lantern light and at the first noise of the wagon, Clark's yard dog set up a racket that had the two women coming out onto the porch. They approached the wagon with swinging storm lanterns.

Hanna Ransom showed a small flash of concerned affection when she saw her husband, wounded and bloody, lying in the hay. I suspected that neither Hanna nor Clark were comfortable with showing affection. She brushed a tear away and said, "Sit up, the two of you. Sarah is bringing a plate of supper for you. Then we'll treat your wounds as best we can and head to Canyon View and the doctor. The rest of you men go into the kitchen and help yourselves."

Hank led the team to the barn and soon emerged with fresh animals.

Hanna Ransom cut the leg off Clark's bloody pants to expose the wound. He yelled that she was ruining a perfectly good pair of pants. "These filthy things were wore out two years ago. I'll be glad to see the end of them."

The bullet wound was inflamed and blue and ugly. Hanna gave it a reasonably tender wash and then said, "You take a grip on something. You ain't going to enjoy this." She then tipped a bottle of liniment directly into the bullet hole. I'm sure Ransom's scream could be heard on the G-bar fifteen miles away. He gripped the side of the wagon box and shuddered with agony, his lips sealed tightly shut to prevent another scream escaping. Hanna wrapped a clean cloth around the leg and said, "You'll be fine. It's just a scratch." Ransom still hadn't caught his breath and by the time he did it was too late to berate Hanna or anyone else.

Sarah had been ministering to Big Bob. His pant leg had also been cut off. His knee was so swollen she had to cut the pant leg up the seam to slip it off. She brought a bucket of cold water and wrapped a wet cloth around the knee. She then used the liniment on the cut on his head. He sucked in a deep breath and balled his hands into fists but didn't make a sound.

Hanna climbed into the back of the wagon and said, "Let's move." Ben was sitting on the wagon seat ready to drive the team.

Hank shook hands around the crew. "Thanks, men. I'll stay here now and let Ma go on to town. Pa will be tied up for a while so I'll be needed. I hope y'all know how much the C/R appreciates your help." With that he stepped to the side of the wagon. He leaned his elbows on the wagon box and looked down at his father. "Ya done good, Pa. You get some doctoring, you'll be back in the saddle in no time."

Clark laid his hand on top of Hank's. "It's good to have

you home, son. Your Ma and I hope you'll stay. We need you." The others around the wagon all studied the ground, wanting to give the family a bit of privacy.

It was nearing morning when we got to the G-bar. The sun was just showing the promise of a clear, fall day. Dora and Laura met us in the yard. Laura had brought Wolf along with her. The dog seemed content no matter where he was. The idea of belonging somewhere didn't seem to be in his thinking at all.

Dora was much more relaxed about showing affection and I was perfectly willing to enjoy every moment of it.

Again, it took but a few minutes for me to catch up a team from the yard pasture and switch them for the tired C/R animals. Ben had been driving the wagon. I rode my horse beside him. In the back, Hanna Ransom was doing her best to comfort both her husband and Big Bob.

Just as Ben was ready to pull out for town, Laura walked up beside the wagon. "Might be best if I was to come along and help your dad. He appears to be hurting mighty bad. You look like you just might go to sleep and drive this wagon into the bush, too. Why don't you sit back and let me take the lines for a while?" Without waiting for an answer, she stepped onto a wheel spoke and lifted herself to the seat. When she reached for the lines, Ben gave them up, not really knowing what else to do. Laura gave him a pleasant smile. "I'll come along and help. Bring the wagon back tomorrow." She somehow managed to put a caring look onto her beautiful face when she looked from Ben to Big Bob. Ben was trapped and he knew it.

As Dora and I stood with our arms around each other, watching the wagon pull for town, Dora looked at Laura. "She's really quite nice but she surely does know how to twist a man around her finger. I'm afraid she has her sights set on Ben. He has no more chance than a snowfall in the desert. I'm glad she didn't set her sights on you. Or maybe she did." It was a statement and a question that I chose to ignore.

As we headed for the house, I said, "Home sure does look good. You're not bad to look at yourself."

She gave me a tighter squeeze. "You need to tell me all about what happened."

"You're not upset with me going?"

"You told me several times on the trail that a man has to do what has to be done. Did you find any more G-bar horses?"

"Found my big red stallion. I'll tell you all about it. After breakfast and about two days of sleep."

We climbed the veranda steps and walked into our beautiful ranch home together.

A LOOK AT MAC'S WAY

Raised in poverty in Missouri, Mac is determined to find a better life for himself and the girl who is still a vague vision in his mind. Work on the Santa Fe Trail, and on a Mississippi River boat give him a start, but the years of Civil War leave him broke and footloose in South Texas. There he discovers more cattle running loose than he ever knew existed. Teaming up with two ex-Federal soldiers, he sets out to gather his wealth, one head at a time.

While gathering and driving Longhorns, Mac and his friends meet an interesting collection of characters, including Margo. Mac and Margo and the crew learn about Longhorns, and life, from hard experience before they eventually head west. Outlaws and harrowing river crossings are just two of the challenges they face along their way.

AVAILABLE NOW FROM REG QUIST AND CKN CHRISTIAN PUBLISHING

ABOUT THE AUTHOR

REG QUIST'S pioneer heritage includes sod shacks, prairie fires, home births, and children's graves under the prairie sod, all working together in the lives of people creating their own space in a new land.

Out of that early generation came farmers, ranchers, business men and women, builders, military graves in faraway lands, Sunday Schools that grew to become churches, plus story tellers, musicians, and much more.

Hard work and self-reliance were the hallmark of those previous great generations, attributes that were absorbed by the following generation.

Quist's career choice took him into the construction world. From heavy industrial work, to construction camps in the remote northern bush, the author emulated his grandfathers, who were both builders, as well as pioneer farmers and ranchers.

Quist's heart was never far from the land. The family photo albums testify to how often he found himself sitting on a horse, both as a child and into later life, when he and his wife owned their own small farm, complete with kids and horses.

Respect for the pioneers, working alongside skilled, tough workmen, and learning from them, marrying his high school sweetheart and welcoming children into the world, purchasing land for the family to grow on, and riding horses with the kids, all melded together to influence Quist's life and writing. Over, and under, and wrapped around his life is Quist's Christian heritage. This too, shows itself in his writing.

Quist's writing career was late in pushing itself forward, remaining a hobby while family and career took precedence. Only in early retirement, was there time for more serious writing.

Quist's writing interests lie in many genres including children's work, short lifestyle stories, cowboy poetry, western novels, plus Christian articles and novels.

Woven through every story is the thought that, even though he was not there himself in that pioneer time, he knew some that were. They are remembered with great respect.